Decided To Live Today

Cover design: Guy Ginsberg
Layout design: Lazar Kackarovski
Proof editor: Brian Cross

ISBN: 978-1-938591-86-0
EISBN: 978-1-938591-87-7

Library of Congress Cataloging-in-Publication data available.

Published by Sole Books and Channel 11 in Los Angeles, California

First edition January 2023

Decided To Live Today

GUY GINSBERG

For Maya & Shira

למאיה ושירה

Contents

1

Carmine

Evangeline is an old bitch who just says things. One of those people who is always spouting off, getting words twisted and then doubling back, jumbling things. She doesn't lie, at least never on purpose, but still, she just talks. People who just talk without thinking are the worst kind of liars because you can't even blame them. No motive. She tells me we're young. That old bitch is lying. I'm old.

My son and his skinny wife put me in this home nine years ago. Here is where I eat good pudding and do my water training. And sometimes rest. I've been here for nine years, watching people ditch their parents at the door, watching poor old schmucks eat pudding and do water training until they pick lint. I think maybe fifty have passed since I've been here, but I'm sure I'm underestimating. I don't even notice anymore. The nurses say I'm well adjusted. The truth is I'm just ready to join them. Today is Sunday and I'm going home. I hope the ride won't be complicated, but the drivers here are all reckless. It's all the cigarettes they do on breaks. Why drivers are allowed to smoke cigarettes before driving helpless old ladies around town is something I will never understand. And on a Sunday no less. I'm in the van now, and it smells like, of course, Phillip Morris the gentile. If I fake a coughing fit maybe I'll get someone fired, but then it might become real and I'll die. Better not take the chance.

I'm not a psychotic like most women my age. I'm also not a liar or a yup. I care about a lot of things, most of them dead, like good music on rare vinyl and my husband. I'm not sentimental but I am for sentiment, unlike the kids today. I can take an ironic story, but the kids live so ironically, and I don't envy the lifestyle. I also don't believe they have a future, but I hope they do.

Today the road to home looks different than it once did, but I'm not the type to act surprised by common change. I do like the way the storm clouds are coming together over the San Fernando; we need the rain. Evangeline, that old hog, is in the van too, probably going to the nail salon or the perfume shop or both. She's up at the front badgering the driver, flirting and thinking she's being cute. What business an 86-year-old woman has being cute, I don't know. Luckily, I think it's making him drive better. God bless that poor bitch.

I'm excited to see home. I haven't been excited in years, and it's exciting to feel excited, even when it's over a little thing like seeing home. I haven't been back since I left and my son sold the place. It's a three bedroom with white banisters, a red Spanish tiled roof, and a garden to make your heart sing. There are a certain number of plants in that garden that don't respond to just anyone, and I'm sure they're all dead, even if the new tenants pay a gardener.

I haven't met the tenants. I don't know them, and I don't much care to know them. As far as I'm concerned, they're just in the way and should mind their business. The home was and still is the best thing I've ever had, and I say that a home is yours until all of you is gone and all that's new is all that's left. I seem to recall a golden retriever named Carmine buried a foot deep in the ground a yard left of the maple tree, and I'm sure the "new tenants" haven't got a clue. So, whose house is it?

Either way, it's just about the only place I could ever picture myself picking lint. To think my son expected me to die on someone else's property — fitting he says he loves his mother. Like I said: the kids, they live ironically. They say it's a Christian country, but I'm no yup. If the Germans had it their way, I'd be mulch for Polish worms. But I had it my way. Coming to America didn't feel like a homecoming, it felt like a due sacrifice — one I was happy to make. I've spent my entire life searching for the right rock to die on. Now I'm here.

The outside looks the same, except they definitely didn't get a gardener for my plants. It's actually better that way, at least they didn't try to change things. Better to let them die. The doorbell is the same, but they didn't get a new Mezuzah, and there's still a rectangle of lighter paint where it used to be. This is still God's house, someone should let them know. A fat woman opens the door for me and I tell her Hi I Am Shoshana I Lived Here From Nineteen Fifty Seven To Nineteen Ninety Three. Can I Come In? and she says Sure. I go into the living room, and the first thing I see is a television set in the corner where I used to do my knitting, and I know it's not my house. But Carmine.

She asks me many silly questions, most of which start with Where or When, like I'm supposed to testify or something. I answer all her questions but come on, let's have some respect for old ladies. The kitchen horrifies me, and I know I shouldn't have even gone in there. Who leaves bread in the drawer below the toaster? If I hear another person tell me they're "practical," I'm going to live longer just to spite them. Practical people keep bread in the freezer where it stays. You keep it in a drawer and it goes stale. Who cares if it's an extra foot from the toaster? People are masochists.

The bedroom scares me too, not because it's different, but because it's exactly the same. They didn't even move the bed. I ask the fat woman if they got a new mattress for it. She says yes, but I sit on it, and I know she's a liar. A masochist liar who lets any stranger sit on her bed. I mean my bed. Her sheets.

So, the bathroom is why I'm here. I tell her I left something in there, and she tells me Wow, It's Been Nine Years, And You Still Remember Where You Left Something, and at Your Age? I mutter something unholy under my breath, remember there's no Mezuzah, then say it louder. Two points for the gentile. Somebody opens the front door, so she goes to check it, leaving me in her bathroom, which is good. In the table under the sink there's a drawer with a bad hinge that stops it from closing all the way, or at least that's what I made my son tell the realtor when he sold the place. But I lied and said the table was a period piece from Poland from my father's house before the war, and we added a clause in the contract that said the new tenant couldn't move or fix it. It's a good enough table, so it stood.

Anyway, in the back where the hinge is supposed to lock in, I tied a little plastic baggy with a key in it, which is why I'm here. I get the key and use it to double lock the bathroom door from the inside. Now, I wait.

The woman knocks and tries opening the door. How's It Going In There? she says, and I don't bother responding. I draw the bath. Her husband, who I guess just arrived, bangs on the door and says he's calling police. I put in a pair of earplugs I got from reception and undress. I dip into the bath once the water is hot enough and high. It's just how I remember it, which is good. I try to relax, but I can still hear the banging, so I dunk my head under the water and hold it there. With the water still running hot and my head just under the tap, I finally feel relaxed. I let my breath go and just stay there.

They say old ladies need other people for everything, but they haven't met the Poles. I have a nice thought about Evangeline, that old bitch, telling rumors about me later today. Maybe she'll accidentally say something true.

2

Serenity is Cheap

The first type of darkness is the darkness behind my eyelids, what I see when I close them. I see it when I sleep, or meditate, or can't bear to look. Possibly also when I blink, though I won't measure that the same way, because the darkness behind a blink is really just the absence of vision, a state best defined by the states that surround it, like the difference between a chalk outline on a gravel road and the body that died there.

The next is the darkness of the night sky I look up at. Or the room I sleep in. Or the movie theater I'm in as it's caught between the last frame of the last trailer (a dancing film I feel no specific way about, but lean over and whisper my half-baked, three-word opinion to my nodding, mouth-breathing co-worker anyway) and the first frame of this movie I've paid too much to come see. When the theater's lights dim, and my eyes hold wide open and still in the patient dark.

The last is true darkness, which I've never seen and never will.

☯☯☯

"We're going to be talking about infinite darkness. It's important that before we begin talking about it, we're both completely aware of what we mean when we say it. Otherwise, we won't be on the same page on this. At all. When I say infinitely dark, what do you think I mean?"

"Darkness that goes on forever. That stretches on everywhere."

"No. The difference between infinite darkness and the dark you just described is that your dark suggests a notion of distance. There is no 'forever' with infinite black, no notion of 'stretching' or 'everywhere.' It's *a*-spatial. *A*-temporal."

"..."

"Meaning that for black to be infinite it must be undetectable. No time, distance, temperature, color, shape, smell, taste — nothing. Infinite."

"OK. Got it."

Now comes a moment without a voice, as Paul Maghene raises his right thumb's knuckle and nail to the part between his lips and exhales slowly against them. He's not convinced.

"Are you sure you got it? I don't want to keep talking only to find out later that we've been referencing different darknesses all along. It would be a total waste of our time," Paul says. "I'm neurotic, I know. Humor me. Give me your revised understanding of infinite darkness."

"Darkness that can't be sensed or measured."

"*Independent* of time and space."

Angus Maghene notices something small and childlike playing in the snow outside, worries it's a naked baby, tenses up, and realizes it's a garden gnome. He takes a big breath and says this: "Wait, but I don't understand. Doesn't the very act of describing it as infinite apply a form of measurement to it?"

"Continue."

"Well, isn't infinity a sort of measurement? Like calling a number with four zeros *a thousand*. Infinity is just *calling* the endless stream of numbers *infinity*. That's what a measurement is, right? A paradox."

Paul considers this comment in two ways. First, as a physicist, he feels an immediate desire to correct his younger brother and move on. But then an itch creeps in, something like respect but not quite. He thinks that his brother's point is really kind of clever, an idea that wouldn't come to most. Wrong as it is, Paul feels a bit touched by his little brother's willingness to question him, so he decides to mix both notions, puts on a sly but genuine smirk, and says this:

"I take your point, and it's a good one. The important idea to throw in here is that a measurement is incomplete without a unit to measure with. Inches, pounds, hours. Measurements require limits. Ends on either side. What you're talking about is a failure of language. The inadequacy of designation. Mathematics is more elegant and precise than even the clearest wording."

As his brother trails off, Angus shifts his gaze onto the empty space between them, now watching specks of dust drift like satellites in orbit. Once again, his brother is right. He's still happy to play along, interjecting whenever he feels that pinched nerve up and behind his left ear urging him to try. He doesn't feel completely shut down by his brother, but definitely doesn't feel encouraged. He's always 51 percent in the loop, just enough to stick around knowing he's better off in than out, though not enough to ever really settle in. He doesn't feel right making the judgment call on whether that's his brother's fault or his own, because he's not totally convinced it's either. Angus nods once, pausing slightly at the bottom of his bow before lifting his heavy head and returning eye contact — his pleasant look only mostly fake.

Paul: "I'm glad you understand. I think we're ready to begin."

Angus agrees: "Let's."

☯ ☯ ☯

It might be of import to note here that Paul cuts himself hamburger style, not hotdog, because he doesn't want to die, he just wants to feel intense and long-lasting pain. He always cuts himself at home, in a half-full bathtub behind a closed bathroom door, locked, with the red and white satchel of cotton balls and bandages in its usual place beneath the kitchen sink, far enough away for him to have to really start feeling the bleeding before he can stop it. Paul lives alone in a Kenwood apartment near UChicago's campus, where he professes.

Hamburger style, just how he folded his first paper airplane in kindergarten, before watching the limp, dopey-looking fighter jet of his imagination meet its match with the air, turn hard left, spiral and mayday disastrously within inches of his excited, hopeful fingers. And the second, and third, until Miss Lorraine came up behind the frustrated toddler hunched over a growing pile of crumpled planes and rotated his next sheet height wise, a gesture of that special grace and elegance known only by those with the utmost finesse. Paul, initially confused and pessimistic that such a small change could alter his luck, was enlightened beyond all doubt as he watched his fourth fighter jet coast like magic in the open air — five, ten, fifteen miles at least before striking Mindy Winters in the ponytail and staying there. The look on his face as he studied the wonder of Miss Lorraine's touch was a cross between joy and perplexity, and although he wouldn't think of it if asked, this was likely the moment when he first became interested in the laws of aerodynamics.

GINSBERG

The cutting came later, when Paul was an undergrad at Johns Hopkins studying physics. He was 19 and away from home, his parents and younger brother carrying on as they were in upstate Illinois, far enough away as to become only an afterthought, pleasant to Facetime if he ever ate lunch alone. Deep down, he probably did love and miss them but was far too privileged to ever feel the urge to remind them, or himself, of that. Most of the time, it was easier to pretend they didn't exist and focus wholly on his work.

Paul started cutting to remind himself he was still alive. All the time he'd spent in physics classes grasping at an abstract, impractical universe caused him to lose touch with what it was really like to be there. The tragic irony being that many young people who spend large parts of their best years in classrooms studying how the universe behaves find themselves less and less able to understand how humans do. This estrangement hits hardest when the world the young physicist professes to know won't stop playing its tricks (for which our world is so famous), like that time Paul's freshman year roommate Rick Mumford, who could barely fill his JHU Swim & Dive speedo and had the reproductive potential of a snow pea, sucked face with the social chair of a top house, or when Theresa Q. Lozenge claimed she could ace the Calc 3 final on three tabs of acid and then *did*; etc., etc..... Or really, whenever that little thing called *chance* pokes its head out and reminds everyone it's still around, and some tribal physicist gets all hot and bothered about how, *technically,* universal equations don't *exactly* account for something called *chance*.... That's when so many of Paul's fresh-faced classmates – would-be astronomers, cosmologists, theorists, and the like – find themselves tragically lost on the road they've begun to pave for themselves, and realize it might be best to give up on the whole physics thing completely – only to later find themselves meddling lazily about as consultants.

Not to be facetious. Physics isn't hard because of Rick Mumford or Theresa Q. Lozenge. It's hard because it's a field of study that badly wants to organize and understand the most difficult thing there is: *everything*. With this, physicists place upon themselves the burden of dissecting and classifying all those little things most other people would simply call magic, or luck, or God.

You might think the difficulty of physics is the time it takes to acquire the requisite knowledge. It's not. The knowledge is the joy. The difficulty is the mindset, a side effect of the knowledge, which requires that the physicist give up on allowing anything to be special just the way it is. A physicist believes all things have an explanation, and all explanations should be found. Love is a neuro-cocktail of norepinephrine, adrenaline, and dopamine. A shooting star is a meteor dissipating to dust in our atmosphere. No physicist worth their weight in quarks would confess that to dissect the most extraordinary things in life is to kill them.

Because, in truth, the more Paul learned about air resistance the less mystical that first flight of the long and thin paper airplane became, and that awesome, inexplicable wonder that first sparked his mind's academic ambition quickly dissipated downwind. This bleak mentality predestined Paul's work never to provide more than an unremitting struggle for fulfillment – a condition that still afflicts him today (and one he unwittingly spreads to his undergraduate students).

But somewhere inside, that boy folding hotdog-style planes still lives, searching for answers in their open wings. Often, the boy comes out just when Paul climbs into the tub and draws the knife, and it pulls him apart. Paul lives in constant imbalance between destruction and discovery, breakthrough and breakdown, and can swing either way on any given day. That's why he cuts.

👀👀👀

"We start with a noo–"

"Wait."

"What?"

"Hold on." Angus pulls out his cellphone.

"Seriously?"

"..."

"I know your generation's average attention span is sub-gerbil but come on. I was about to get into it," Paul says, wide-eyed and stiff.

"One sec... there," as Pink Floyd's "Brain Damage" starts to play loudly from his phone's speakers.

"Seriously?"

"Come on. It's appropriate."

"How is music appropriate when we're trying to talk?"

"It's *Dark Side*."

"..."

"*Of The Moon*. We're talking about space. It's theme music."

"You're absurd."

"*You're* absurd."

"Fine. I'm absurd. At least lower the volume."

Angus cuts the song to half blast. "Happy?"

"I was never unhappy. Just wish you would involve yourself a bit more in the conversation is all. I'm trying to explain something interesting, something you might actually understand."

"You wish..."

"..."

"Wish I Was Here?"

"Wow."

"Alright. Sorry. I'm listening."

"It's OK."

"Go ahead."

"I was going to."

"Alright."

Paul and Angus have been riding for the past fifteen minutes on a Metra NCS train from Chicago to Antioch, and Angus is facing opposite the train's motion. It's bright outside, but the brothers are dressed for the winter. Paul is looking at Angus, and Angus is looking out the window, his eyes locked on the sun's blinding reflection off snow.

"We start with a noodle," Paul finally gets to say.

"Right."

"Well, I guess it doesn't quite start there, but it's a good entry point..."

"Sure."

"For us. So, what do you think would happen if you dove into a black hole?" Paul half-smirks as he says this.

"Would I start with a noodle?"

"You'd actually end with one. As one." Half-smirk grows full.

"Right."

"..."

"What does that mean?"

"Exactly. What does that mean? So, the first thing you need to know about black holes is that there are two rare kinds and two common kinds. We'll stick to the common. Stellar and supermassive."

"What about massive?"

"No massive."

"So, they just skipped massive and went straight for supermassive?"

"Well, these are really *really* massive black holes. To call them just massive would do them an injustice."

"How massive are we talking?"

"Well, for instance, the one in the middle of the Milky Way, Sagittarius A-star, is four million times more massive than the sun."

"Woah. That's like..."

"Not even close to the biggest one found."

"*Super. Massive.*"

The train track is rickety at times but mostly smooth. Angus tries to avoid eye contact, but is worried that Paul knows he's intentionally avoiding it because there's nothing but snow to see outside.

"Exactly. So, we think there's probably a supermassive black hole at the center of most galaxies in the universe. Jury's still out on how they got there. But we observe them in most."

"Wait."

"I know what you're going to ask."

"Right."

"We can't observe them because they're infinitely dark. The whole point of black holes is that the gravity in the center of each one is so strong that not even light escapes its inward suck. They're literally impossible to observe directly. Totally invisible. So, we observe them by their impact on the stuff around them."

"Sure."

"So, when anything gets too close to a black hole, it gets sucked in and disappears."

"Some might say slurped. Like a noodle."

"Exactly. So, let's say you're an astronaut and dive headfirst into a black hole."

"Naturally."

"Naturally. So, because of something called *the gravitational gradient*," Paul chews out the words like they're dried fruit, "which *basically* means that the closer to the center of the black hole you go, the stronger the gravity becomes, your body would get stretched like spaghetti. Diving headfirst, the gravity at your head would be way stronger than at your feet."

"Huh."

"You'd be pulled at the poles. Spaghettified. Same thing goes for stars."

"Astro-Angus."

"Long and thin."

"Noodle-naut."

"And dead."

"..."

"..."

"So where do the things come from?"

"Still an open question. Origin unknown, though there's constant research. Some say they're stellar black holes that grow over time as they suck in more stuff."

"..."

"..."

"*Stellar.*"

"Stellar black holes. The other kind. They show up after a supernova."

"..."

"Which is when a star collapses in on itself."

"..."

"A massive explosion leaves behind a carcass of super gravity where no light escapes."

"..."

"A black hole."

"Ah."

"Exactly."

"Going out with a bang."

"Yes."

"Take the star, leave the cannoli."

"..."

"Invisible cannoli."

"..."

"Attracts Italians from all corners of the galaxy."

"Angus."

"Boopity Yappity Invisible Cannoli. Scoopity Doopity Astro Spaghetti."

"Look at me."

"Don Vincenzo's Space Bistro. Astro Spaghetti."

"Angus."

"Donny V's Spaghetti and Spaceballs."

"Look at me."

"I am."

"You're looking out the window and have been this whole time."

"Have I?"

"Still are."

"Sorry. The scenery. It distracts."

"Angus."

"The snow is so white. Blinding."

"Look at me."

"I can't take my eyes off it. They won't re-adjust right. I just know they won't."

"I cut myself."

"I just know it. They won't re-adjust right in this dark train, so I'm deadlocked."

"I've cut myself since sophomore year at Johns."

"Deadlocked on the blinding snow, I tell you."

"I hide it from dad and you because I'm worried you'll think I'm depressed and won't want me to keep working."

"..."

"Do you care?"

"..."

"Look at me."

"I can't. My eyes."

"Look at me, Angus."

"My eyes."

"Look."

"The snow."

Paul grabs Angus by the head and pulls his gaze toward him. Angus jerks to pull off his brother's hands, but they're immovable, freeze-dried to his face. Paul says nothing as he holds his brother there. The train still rolls, although seemingly slower than it had been before. Angus struggles to refocus his eyes on his brother and, for a few moments, sees nothing but an inward-creeping brightness, the side effect of white light imprinted on his vision. As his eyes train onto his brother's face, he sees him clearly for what feels like the first time in years. This is the first time they've touched in as long as Angus can remember. Paul is a shaken boy, crying as he never has, his soppy nose just inches from his baby brother's face, eyes depthless and glazed.

"I'm not ready to see her," Paul says.

Angus says nothing, but thinks the same.

The difference between darknesses is best understood from how they arise. The first kind, A-dark, the kind that lives behind my eyelids, is always there, waiting for my call. Unlike the third, C-dark, the truest kind, which too waits under light's cover, A-dark is mine to form. C-dark is more encompassing, existing independent of me: it is light's counterweight. B-dark, the darkness seen through open eyes, is necessarily temporary. It depends on nothing more than the darkness of my world and how much attention I give it.

The overlap between darknesses A, B, and C is where I lose myself. What if they're all manifestations of one darkness, and I am fabricating imaginary differences between them for convenience? The only seemingly logical difference I can see between A-dark and B-dark is the imbalance between control and imposition. A-dark is mine. I find it myself when I *choose* to close my eyes. A-dark only exists because I exist and can close my eyes.

On the other hand, B-dark is outside my reach, how a hall with no windows or lights is still dark even after I open my eyes. Though how could I know, in a totally dark room, whether my eyes are open or closed? Feeling aside, is there a distinction to be made between the darkness that exists dependent and independent of me? Meaning, can I control the darkness even *after* it's been imposed on me? And if so, does this subsume B-dark into a more comprehensive AB-dark? I have only questions, and it seems no answer.

C-dark is the most difficult, and attempting to understand it often feels like an utterly pointless endeavor. If A and B-dark are the physical emergence of darkness, C-dark is the form. Truthfully, I only speculate on its existence as it complements the light I can see. This, the "true" and "infinite" darkness, must live outside the realm of light that can be seen, the way that *nothing* only exists because *something* does. But I have never seen *nothing*. I have no conception of what *nothing* really is (given it *is* anything at all). I only conceptualize it as it relates to *something*, which defeats its entire purpose. In theory, C-dark should be the essence of darkness, home for the other two forms – but its existence is uncertain, or worse, an illusion.

I sometimes worry that I haven't the slightest clue what I'm working toward. But I also know that infinite darkness is necessarily *that which cannot be directly observed*. Does this mean that my inability to understand it is its very own proof? That's too easy an explanation, never mind a convolution. Just because I may never know what exactly I'm looking for doesn't mean I've found it. Maybe it's all just a trick of language. Maybe it's not.

Oh well. The bath is getting cold.

Angus works wood with his and Paul's dad, Oliver-James, a Methodist, four days a week at their shop in Antioch. Angus mostly carves, since Dad got rheumatoid arthritis and can't grip a gouge without a wince. His is the carving station up front facing the window, which he pushed tight against the glass, so when the sun rises, it floods. He doesn't have to get into the shop until eight but likes to have his coffee and potato danish at his desk, where he can watch the dawn shadows get tall off his upright tools. The morning sun is a routine he can trust, plus it's warm, even in winter.

After coffee, Angus will work on whatever he's been doing, usually drawer or door faces, a nightstand's trim or its specialty feet. He'll watch Dad arrive from the window, and with wandering eyes they'll lose a few minutes finishing the conversation they couldn't the day before. Oliver-James is a passionate speaker on even the most routine subjects, often rambling for minutes about the morning's bitter wind or an overwarm teacup he burnt a lip on. Angus tosses a moan or a head nod when need be but generally is okay with just listening to Dad go on. Oliver-James wasn't always a big talker, but turned so once he lost the power to speak with his tools, and both he and Angus sort of carry that weight.

He's special with the carver's pencil, Angus is, a V-shaped tool for details and outlining that dad passed down when he could no longer steady it. When he carves, he pays special attention to the curled shavings that come out of the wood, judging his progress by their thickness and bend – not the imprints they leave behind. Like all other woodworking knowledge he's got, Angus picked this quirk up from Dad, who's told Angus repeatedly to pick his eyes up from the tool's tip and watch the shavings dance instead. Because, he always says, there's more to learn about woodwork from what's removed than what remains.

The train's window has mostly frosted over from the edges in, and its numbing surface against Paul's leaning temple feels just right.

"Why do you always make things so complicated?" Angus says.

"I don't know," Paul replies.

"You're just like Dad."

"Am I?"

"With your overthinking and your worrying. Dad's the same ever since he stopped working."

"Dad still works."

"No, he doesn't, he just watches me carve. He blames his hands. I can feel his eyes on me when I'm working, and it slows me down."

"I didn't know that."

"You'd know if you ever came to visit. He hasn't made a thing in two years."

"..."

"Which I'm not trying to guilt you about. I know you're busy."

"I'm not."

"Of course you are. You have your students and your black hole work. It's hard to do it all."

"Sure, it's hard. But I haven't done anything. It's actually hard *because* I haven't done anything. I can't even remember the last thing I did that I felt proud of. The last thing I did that I *felt* at all. It's like I'm chasing my own tail with everything I do. My work, my life. You and dad."

"Paul, you're focused on all the wrong things."

"I know."

Woodworking is a refined practice that requires intense focus and meticulous care to do well, but Oliver-James knows it's also a characteristically human undertaking. If there is any objective truth about woodworking he can see, it's that the uncut, living tree is the most spectacularly sculpted form there is. Carving is to take the naturally grown tree and constrain it, rob it of its structural integrity and compel it to fit one's subjective, human taste. To cut the tree, sand, section, mold, and carve it are shameless acts in a tragic play called the imposition of will. Yet, when Angus takes his carver's pencil to the oak plank, he thinks not of the essence of wood, but of how to efficiently use the skills he's picked up over the years working it. In a way, he's nested himself between the meta and the physical and called it home. It's a conveniently meaningful life.

The sad truth is that what Angus really does is create human value by corrupting natural value. Oliver-James knows it now, but not before his hands forced him to take a step back and reflect. He's actually quite lucky that he never realized his plight while still able to work. So how could Angus know? All he does is carve. To correct his son's misunderstanding and show him the futility of his efforts would steal the purpose from his life. Because the truth is, Angus needs his ignorance like he needs the morning sun's long shadows. So Oliver-James says nothing, only reminding his son to watch the shavings grow, hoping he'll find it himself.

The sun rises higher and higher into the sky, hovering almost directly over the running train as it slows to its stop in Antioch. Angus gets up first, and then Paul, and they exit the train. The platform they walk on wasn't properly salted before the snow fell, and is covered with a thin coat of ice. Paul yells to be heard over the wind spilling across his face.

"When was the last time you spoke to her?"

"Two days before. You?"

"I can't remember. I think my 23rd birthday. She called me. I could be wrong."

They turn at the platform's edge and start up a snow-covered hill. A thin cloud hides the sun as they climb, and the wet snow on the ground overpowers Paul's thin city shoes. His wet socks make him uncomfortable, and he struggles not to think about it. Angus reaches the hilltop first and stops to wait for his brother, and when Paul reaches the top, the sun peeks out from behind the cloud, now directly above them in the sky. They cross over a low metal gate and reach a maze of powdered headstones. Angus leads the way.

"It's going to be hard to find her, with the snow," Angus says.

"Should we come back another day?" Paul replies.

"It's alright."

With the sun directly overhead, the stones are all shadowless. Mom is somewhere underneath them, waiting for her boys. Angus and Paul walk in parallel, their heads scanning the snow in opposite directions. Together, they will soon find her. There is only the day's blinding white to comb through.

3

An Unofficial Explanation for Just Why We Say Chop And Lop

It has become wholly evident through one minute of surface level Google searching that there is a clear and undeniable relationship between *chop* as it serves both the purpose of a slang term for BONG RIP, as a verb/noun referring somewhat ubiquitously to the act of something being cut into smaller pieces, and *lop*. I say somewhat as not to disregard the presence of *chop* in its same form as a noun describing what many dub a KARATE-CHOP, a downward attack move used in mixed or unmixed martial arts that is carried out by the thrust force of the side of one's hand against the body of an object, said object rarely not being another human being or for training's sake a pad or block of wood. It may also refer to a cut of pork-loin.

Lop on the other hand of the same dictionary-skewed man can be defined as a verb/noun referring to a branch or, in rare cases, another object connected to a tree that is being cut or has been cut down. An example of which used in a sentence is, "she lopped off more branches than she could chew."

So, what is there to say of two words with similar phonetic sounds that mean more or less the same thing (to cut) and their relationship with the BONG RIP?

Things may be cut away, cut through, cut with, cut against, cut for, cut loose, cut in half, cut in squares, cut into pieces. However, my main argument in this short paper concerns the ability for something to be *cut off*, much like the head of a well-shit-I-fucked-up dictator or an ill-audienced statement. But the cutting off I'll be discussing is more so one of mental attachment to reality. The cutting-off of one's presence, or soul in the matter, from the matters at hand which make them human. One's connection to this spirit, or soul, or will to be, is what connects the internal with the external, the shielded with the brazen. For many reasons, it's appealing to "cut yourself off" from a situation, whether that situation be stress-inducing or feared. Cutting off from these situations can be cathartic and therapeutic, making the cutter/cutee feel better distanced from the pain. The pain of existence – an unexplainable attachment to both our physical being as well as our perception that this being should be guarded against impurities that pose a threat to our manicured comfort – is what we both fear the most and hold most dear to our hearts. We cut ourselves off from our attachment to our existence to free ourselves from its pain, while still hanging from the thread of being that gives us the will to stay alive. How so, if to live is to feel pain, do we stay alive? If the pain were constant, perhaps we would seek constant ends, but because the pain can be comfortably shifted away like a big book we don't want to read and replaced by a candy bar, or a 24-hour marathon of *Friends* on TV, or maybe, I don't know, something like a 15'-21' glass pipe, filled with nothing but the freshest distilled water and more or less 8' of glass tubing leading up to nothing but the best and finest diced herbs cut and pressed into a glass bowl inserted into glass tubing which rests comfortably submerged in distilled water that sits at the basin of the pipe and awaits the warm, milky fill of smoke to pass into it, through it, and away from it as slowly and with as much *jus* as the person sucking it through can muster, then maybe we don't have to be afraid right now. These impermanent ends, allowing us to cut ourselves off from the true reality of our misguided perception, allow the dark annals of our brain that tell us, hey, maybe today's the day it all ends because there's really no running, but hey, hey, I'm talking here, hey, hey, quit trying to shut me up, don't shut me up, hey, hey, hey man! You're a superhero. You're flying!

4

Excerpts from "Color Is Added"

A novel I will never finish

Morning Wood

Impoverished Julius Wood wasn't always impoverished. Only recently, after releasing himself from his sixth menial job in the last two years, for the third time through an unbodied email message's subject line, Wood truly let himself loose of his proverbial shackles. Performing tasks in exchange for money, which to him represented both a Faust-like contractual death sentence and a willful acceptance into "The System," was simply an utter waste of time. Not jobs or work in general, but just the idea of Wood actually *performing* in one; Wood the kind of worker who never seemed to fully realize the position he took, making each of his somehow held jobs meld into the same sort of thing. Like no matter where you put the guy – whether it's hunched over bubbling fries at The Outback or hunched out back under two by fours – he was still filled to the brim with the effervescent nonchalance of a six-year-old with an iPad. The kind of guy who wore loose jeans that were too long and sort of hugged around the heels of his sneakers, getting just tremendously dirty under there, painfully exposed to whatever it was his shoes were made to deal with, turning mug brown with muggier darker brown where dirt got really in there, engraved with specks of rock and sand so deep they started to look less like blue jeans and more like rocky-road ice cream. The kind of guy who'd always clip his menial name tag to a spot on his body where nobody wanted or needed to look, like his back pocket or the brim of his backward hat. The kind of guy who just morphed into the cooking counter when there was nobody to service, possibly magnetized by his butt tag to the shiny metallic surfaces (which were so stained and reddened with food juice that they didn't do his rocky road jeans any favors). But still, Wood always seemed to know less about his position than was even anticipated, maybe even unsure what it meant to hold a position at all, like he just limped into the job without warning and immediately fell asleep.

His third of six bosses in the last 24 months, tacky Tammy Wallerby over at The Outback, where they make steaks almost purely to remind you you're poor, basically had to strap herself to Wood and wear him like an exoskeleton just to get the buns in the proverbial oven. This, for a couple of weeks before realizing that every time she turned her back Wood would just doze off, quite literally fall asleep within seconds of ditching her attention, and just sort of hover there over the bubbling potato sticks as they got crispier and crispier, not even shaking his nose at the crescendoing burn smell, and have to be jolted awake not by tacky flimsy Tammy but by Pierre or Guadalupe, or even poked in the ribs with a mop stick by one of the janitorial help. Then, finally realizing how amazingly useless Wood was, disgracing even the menial work of a fry cook, Wallerby dramatically shifted her own character, wore her tacky flimsy self like an exoskeleton, strapped in and told Wood to nut up or piss off, to which Wood replied almost without even opening his mouth, "Buhbyeeee." This, which fit evenly with Wood's track record of quitting a job only to fall like a perfectly spawned Tetris block into the next, fit rather unevenly with Tammy Wallerby, who'd gone so far out of her comfort zone to confront Wood that the inevitable failure of her confrontation and the feelings of intense self-loathing and fear that came next became just too much for her tacky flimsy self to bare, resulting in a rather unkosher relapse into opioid use – to somehow bring her shattered self together – as she sorely misjudged the psycho-friendly effectiveness of snorting leftover Adderall from her last opiate dive on the reddened, stained metallic countertops of her pasty and unassuming Outback Home of Steak.

So Wood, who'd gone on pretty much just like that for the better part of 104 weeks since being capped and gowned out of Harvard Westlake HS, and ditched for both economic and familial good by the Greater Wood's as a delinquent without sustainable habits or promising futures, found himself once again careless and free to live by his own devices – which more or less meant bottom feeding off his pal Kirk, who was still more or less bottom feeding off his own self-loathing Greaters. But Kirk – who inhabited a soggy black hole with one high square window in the attic of the Greater Kirk's 16th century Gothic castle in Holmby Hills, which quite literally featured twin guard towers in the north and southeast corners, not to mention an ever-loving *moat* circling the place that reeked forcefully of garlicky phosphorus – was totally and spiritually cool with the boy Julius kicking back and resting assured on the financed futon by the lamplight, even though occasionally,

Kirk thought important to let Wood know, he would need the space where the lamp was, because he read somewhere online that it's bad for your eyes to look at smartphones in total darkness.

The dark space where Kirk spends his evenings to nights, and where Wood spent his full days for weeks before doom, is a stretched, diamond-shaped attic with wood ceiling panels and plank flooring that certainly isn't oak, but exudes an oaky vibe that comforts Kirk some. The claustrophobic diagonal walls that make it necessary to kneel in the room's four corners remind Wood of the scene in Star Wars where the Death Star's garbage shoot walls slowly close in on all the good guys, and Kirk's walls are tapestried with faux far-east type sheets of orange and lime green with buddhisty shapes that sag in the middle and make the room feel even smaller. The rug in the room's focus is one of those that you wouldn't dare wear shoes on, milk-white with the furry cotton ball fuzz that absolutely *eats* dirt and hair and is impossible to clean once dirtied, only this one so tested by bong time that its fickle hair is garnished with so many weed crumbs that the clinically baked Jackie Rosenstein once called the rug *Grinch*.

The rug acts as the attic's holy ground, and the 21-inch water pipe at its core is its altar. Kirk prays (rips bong) to The Lord (to get toasted) anywhere between three and seven independent times a day, almost always with friends, who flow in and out of his space like particles diffusing from an area of low concentration to an area higher. These friends of Kirk, maybe six or seven independent faces, of which Wood knows the name of maybe half, seem never to arrive at Kirk's with any sort of intentions at all, totally devoid of all meaning and purpose, no more than zombies stuck in loops coming in and going out around the same time every day. Wood sometimes wonders if these people even form independent thoughts, if they even make the conscious decision to go to Kirk's that day at all, or if they just live on autopilot, gassed up, Kirk's spot a necessary item on their daily to-do list (which Wood knows they don't have, but likes to imagine the ridiculous contents of if they did).

And now, so barely June 4th that Kirk hasn't even yet woken for his breakfast (which is served all day) shift at Denny's in Westwood Village, and the rising sun pierces in thin beams through the paneled, angled ceiling and sheds light on the attic's heavily dusted airspace, and millions of speckled particles can be seen gravitating through the room like a Kubrick spacecraft, a chunk of floor is swallowed by the level below as the attic door is pulled open and the ladder retracted, disrupting the air flow in the room and sending spacecraft bouncing every which way. The noise of this wakes Wood alone, as he lays on his left side, and he peers his higher right eye over to the ghastly fluorescent light, that now floods the otherwise naturally black attic, and hears slow, creaky steps. These steps, each one creakier than the last, are almost mind-bendingly slow, with a total moment of silence between each impending creak. Wood, fully awake now and in serious awe of the soul-crushing pace of *whoever-the-fuck* needs to come up right now, rises to his feet and rushes to the opening, creating speedy and loud thumping creaks that combine to make bed-squeak music with the visitor's slow, soft ones. But before he reaches the hole, a head pokes halfway into the attic, blond hair half lit from behind followed by gray bug eyes which scan the room robotically, and Wood stops in his tracts and sighs a big sigh before turning back to bed and hitting the futon with empty gravitational force. A loud thump. The uninvited guest laughs a silent, airy laugh as he hoists himself up. He whispers to no one: *Timber.*

"Mmm," grunts Wood, not currently akin to puns, especially when coming from Ricky Max, the doubly first named twat who Julius takes personal offense with. After carefully shutting the attic door so as not to wake Kirk, Max heads to the altar to begin the morning ritual.

"Kirkus sure is keeshed," Max observes. "Shlumped. Out. Done for."

Head lifting from the pillow, swiveling to face Max like a movie monster and thwacking back down, Julius opines: "It's too early."

Exchanging whispers. "That's why they call it a wake 'n bake J-box. Don't @ me."

"None of that was English."

'The drawbridge was down, so I let myself in. Don't worry boss, Kirkus and I are superchillin'. I'll be in and out.'

'Mmm.' The head swivels back; the eyes tighten.

Julius knows Ricky Max as a suspiciously colorful character. He's always got on aggressively yellow shoes that squeak, not to mention those godforsaken tank tops. He's always describing things as "scrumptious" and rubbing clean the brims of bongs with his shirt before smoking them. He's got that faux chill vibe of a New Yorker in Los Angeles but really hails from south Florida, which makes almost *more* sense. But what makes Julius most suspicious is the rectangle of maroonish brown fuzz on the guy's upper lip that alludes to nothing more than sheer mystery. Mustaches aren't typically alarming to Wood, but the thing about Max is that he's utterly hairless everywhere but the dome and the 'stache. His arms and legs are shiny like marble countertops, and his pits – always in view due to god-forsaken tank tops – are like empty bowls. Not even the prickly dots of a shaven pit, no remnants of hair that might have been, simply clear skin. So how, Wood wonders, does he carry such 'stache? And why, more importantly, is it a different color than his surfer blond hair? The facts just don't add up regarding Max, adding to his reputation as Julius' least favorite attic presence whether or not it's still disgustingly A.M. Plus, Max is currently rubbing clean the brim of a bong he hasn't seen anyone use, putting to work the loose front tail of his crystal blue tank as a washcloth, not even considering the possibility that it's actually dirtier than the bong itself.

At what point will Darwinism mean *not* continuing the human race? In the sense that until now, the most well-defined purpose for humanity has been the perpetuation of more humanity, Wood's scientific mind understanding that the main core driver of human existence is to spin the cog, make it happen, realize the dream: multiply. With intentions as pure as to secure the World Domination bag, pass forth one's loins to a fresher generation, who in themselves soon must sus out the governing concept, freeze the mustard, keep it fresh: reproduce.

Max crumbles greens into a Santa Cruz Shredder he copped from his cousin Lewis and twists the top like a bottle cap twice, thrice, quattrice before unloading the grinder's freshly powdered snowpack into the bong's 5-hole bowl, stuffing it tight and sprinkling a hefty dash of tobacco on top like he's seasoning a tasteless steak. The glass pipe's water is so browned and swampy it's a miracle of group negligence that nobody's given it a quick hard rinse, each ripper fully expecting Kirk to handle his business, Kirk half expecting one of them to get bothered enough to sub-in.

But of course, with population levels dramatically rising to what will frighteningly soon be unsustainable numbers, food & water & territorial capacity wise, the internal drive is facing a serious dilemma way down deep, the eternal *man v. himself* motif. Forever it's made the most sense to just pop 'em out like candy, sustain the self with more selves, rely on the young to guard and protect the old. But at what point will the resources available be so scarce, so personable, and so immediate that it makes more survival sense to reel the whole reproduction thing way in? Call it quits? Have your cake, eat it, and save the tray for seconds?

Ricky Max, now chugging like a choo-choo, sparked up and riding this train 'til the last stop, a milky barrel of smoke slowly rising until the moment it meets his puckered lips, greeting them, accepting them as their consumer, becoming whole. It doesn't take long for this process of consumption and release to come to a close, leaving Ricky in a momentary fit of internal despair as he politely holds a cough to maintain the silence, and then a longer-lasting spring of internal completion as the smoke finds its way home, takes its shoes off at the door, settles into bed.

The aforementioned not-too-distant Darwinistic paradox is what Wood dreams of for something less than 10 minutes, writhing futon-wise with a discomfort that's almost rhythmic, until the release and crank of the attic door shutting stirs him back awake. Max's leftover smoke hovers like the imprint of a thundercloud in the damp, oaky attic, partially illuminated by falling spears of brilliance, cutting through the tattered ceiling, quickly dissipating to nothing.

So Tired of Being Alone

Of course, the problem with having sex with someone you're not even pretending to love is that once it's all through and you've locked the door behind her, scrubbed yourself to death in the shower, put on a new pair of underpants and changed your sheets, you're hit with that severe head to toe loneliness that all but knocks you on your existential ass. The kind of loneliness that manifests in a full-body emptiness, like the girl who's just come and gone has emptied you of much more than what you thought. It's a dread wholly separate from any other type of loneliness because it can't be cured by other people; it's a loneliness that starts and ends within.

This type of post-loveless-coitus loneliness pulls your eyes out of your head and spins them around, so you get a good look at the sorry mess of yourself you've become (with the help of another seriously lonely human being), and once they (your eyes) turn back around and plop back into their sockets, you feel like a stranger in your own body. You start to despise the person you just gave yourself away to and run circles in your head trying to find ways to blame them. But it's in you now, whether it's their fault or yours, and deep down, you know that it's impossible to be faultless, a la – "it takes two to tango." Still, it makes you immediately disgusted by the person you've just tangoed with, as they morph from sexy, attainable, and worth it to drawn-out, weak, colorless.

The worst of it is the immediacy. It onsets just as you pull out and lay back on the bed, it festers in the back of your mind as you clean yourself, it builds as you change your clothes, and it whacks you over the fucking head the second your partner shoves off.

This thundercloud of dread weighs you down like a heavy book bag, and is only ever cured by getting back into the bed on the sheets you've just laid, crawling up in the fetal position, and rocking your mind to a complimentary emptiness – until it can't be distinguished from the rest of your body. Only once the mind is blank and shut down can you start to heal from this emptiness, because everything reminds you of it – and the only way to escape it is to just stop thinking completely. It goes without saying that you don't want to look in the mirror when you feel this type of loneliness, because it's most evident in, and hardest on, the eyes.

But so only once your mind and body become void, and you're rocking yourself toward a weary dreamless sleep on your fresh white sheets, can you start to slowly, piece by piece, become whole again, as your mind reattaches to your body – which still feels sticky icky regardless of how ferociously it's been washed. Then you sleep, and in your dreams, you begin to recover and forget what you can about the soul-sucking demon who just stole your purity and walked out that door clasping it in their teeth. You wake up feeling tired and sad but together, capable of functioning that day without total body-mind failure as your head starts to escape the hole it dug trying to reclaim your body. Except once you settle into yourself again, you can't help but consider her, and how she's feeling, and you're reminded of the fact that *she too did tango*, and you're plagued with the idea that she likely feels just as empty and lonely as you do or worse, because she had the even more soul-sucking walk to her car and drive home before she could clean off the filth *you* bestowed upon *her*, and had to rock *herself* into a weary dreamless sleep... and you relearn to tango all by yourself, and you hope and pray that she doesn't feel about you the way you feel about her, and you maybe even start to feel sorry.

But the day goes on, and then a full week passes, and by then you've more or less completely recycled and reconnected your body with your mind and become whole again. Then, just as the color starts to come back to your eyes, your phone lights up – a message from her – asking *what are you up to tonight?* and you again become who you've always been.

5

Leaf

A leaf crunches under foot. Dry. It is autumn; the leaf had died and fallen before it was crunched. The leaf was already dead. The foot had nothing to do with it.

The foot is alive and moves, crunching dead leaves with every step, but taking no blame. The leaves were already dead. The foot continues to step; there is no remorse for the foot, for the leaves were already dead. The foot continues.

The foot is wrapped in socks, which are themselves wrapped in shoe. Two protective layers, each one stronger than the last. The foot has no ears; the foot can only touch. The foot doesn't touch the leaves it crunches. The foot has no ears, and the shoe is cushioned and protective. The foot knows nothing of the leaves it crunches. To the foot, the leaves are nonexistent. The leaves are negligible, at least for the foot. At least for the foot wearing protective layers.

But the leaves were dead already. The foot had nothing to do with it. The foot is as negligible to the dead leaf as the dead leaf is to the foot. Still so, a leaf crunches under foot.

The foot keeps moving, connected to a leg that carries it along. The leg needs the foot as much as the foot needs the leg. Neither needs the leaf, but neither even knows the leaf exists. There are protective layers.

The layers on the foot and leg are attached to a woman, using her leg to move forward. The leg and the woman need each other to move forward as one. Without a woman, there is no moving leg, and without moving legs, the woman cannot move forward as one. A woman without a moving leg can move forward, but not without help from another. To move as one, the leg and the feet are needed. The protective layers are not.

To move forward as one, the woman must will herself forward. She does this with her mind, which can only will forward her leg and her foot when they are with her. A mind cannot control the leg or foot of another. Together, the leg and the foot and the woman are one. The purpose of this one is to move forward.

The woman has ears and can hear the leaves crunching underfoot. She knows it is her foot crunching the leaves because the sound of the crunching leaf is distinct and is tied to the step of her foot. The sound she hears when her foot crunches the leaf makes her foot and the leaf come together as one. They are one because together, they make the sound that she hears. The oneness is the sound.

The woman doesn't fear this sound, or take shame or blame in this sound, which she knows is due to the oneness of her stepping foot and the dead leaf. This is because the leaf was already dead. Her foot did not cause the death of the leaf, it only crunched a dead thing. Her foot is not a killer. She is not a killer. She is only a producer of sound. In this way, she is a creator. A creator of sound.

The woman doesn't notice she has become a creator, because while she hears the sound that her foot makes when it crunches the leaf, she doesn't internalize that this has made her a creator. Her mind is elsewhere. Her mind is occupied with things that do not concern herself as the creator of this sound. Although her mind is unaware she is a creator, she is not a killer. The leaves were dead already.

The leaves don't know they are crunched by an absent-minded woman's foot. They are dead already. The leaves know nothing at all. They do not even know the sound they make when crunched by the woman's foot. They are creators of sound who are already dead. Because they are dead, they will never know that they have become creators of sound. They will never know that when they become one with the step of a foot, they become creators.

The creator of sound is not the foot, for the foot needs the leaf. The creator of sound is not the leaf, for it needs the foot. Sound is only created when the foot and the leaf become one. Together, they are creators. Though neither will know of the sound they have created, for the foot has no ears, and the leaves are already dead.

The woman is the only one around who can hear the sound that her foot and the leaf that it crunches have created, but her mind is elsewhere. Her mind considers feelings and thoughts more profound than the sound created when a leaf crunches under a foot.

Had the woman been conscious of her foot, the leaf that it crunches, and the sound that this unison created, she would have thought about it. This thought, while only in her mind, would have existed. Because this thought and recognition of sound would exist, it would qualify that the sound had too existed. Her thinking of the sound would have given the sound a purpose. Her thinking of the sound would have given meaning to the unison between leaf and foot.

If only to be considered by someone, the creators of sound have found meaning. To be considered.

But the woman is not conscious; she does not consider this. Her mind is too profound.

And really, what is "meaning" for a leaf that is already dead?

What is "purpose" to a foot which is wrapped in protective layers and cannot sense its creation? A foot which is carried along by a leg attached to a woman who is unconscious of her foot's creation?

The leaf and the foot feel no anger toward the woman for neglecting to provide them with purpose. The leaf is already dead, and the foot has moved on, connected to a moving leg attached to a woman alive. Alive, although unconscious. Alive, although seemingly already dead.

The leaf had nothing to do with it.

The Endless Shitter
or, We Are All Turkey

"I'm at Fordham University in the City," is something I've become accustomed to spitting robotically on brooding faces I barely remember, who always bask in my accomplishments like a warm light and breath *ooh* or *ahh* because isn't it impressive?

"And what are you studying?" is without fail the follow-up question that I know can be answered along with the first response, but I've realized is better clung on to for prolonging the conversation to a socially acceptable length. By no means do I truly want to prolong these conversations, but cutting the small talk into intervals makes it more normal when one of us trails off and goes away to twist a lightbulb.

"Biomedical engineering, with a concentration on annulation," is something I have never thought about studying with a concentration on something nonexistent I read about in more depth than I would have liked in *Infinite Jest*. I really don't know anything about either, but it does me the dual service of confusing and impressing the already affected listener. I've found there isn't much left for them to say when they're both confused and impressed.

"That sounds interesting! Say, remind me, who are your folks again?"

"Louis and Jane Johns, from Lancaster."

"Oh! We just met them by the pool table. Honey, this is the Johns' boy, Kyle. That's what they said their boy's name was, right Kyle?"

"You have a good memory, sir."

"Oh! Not great, just good enough."

"Ah."

Mr. *Ooh* poked at the ice in his drink with his cocktail straw before muttering into his mustache and skipping toward the nearest lightbulb. People at gatherings are like pests in the way they attract to the brightest light. This particular *Ooh* was less particular than most. Dry and lifeless, like someone hanging by the rope of their heyday. He reminded me of Robert De Niro's character in Jackie Brown if he were less cool. Like a man wilted. A man who thought good meant great, and looked like it.

My family, like many immigrant families, doesn't do intimate Thanksgiving. This is both good and bad. Bad because of the daunting small talk that gatherings bring. Good because we typically will end up in a house much nicer than ours, eating food much better than ours, engaging in conversation much easier than ours. Only two families invite my family to Thanksgiving; one has a pool table and the other has a pool. In my house, there is a pendulum clock. We're at pool table house this Thanksgiving, and if my memory is any good, I'd say the pool house family is here too. It's that sort of deal.

This house looks built for a movie instead of a family. All the walls are curved but none of the rooms are circular, which is as involved in trigonometry as I'm willing to get. There are drapes over doors that open into rooms that are just foyers for other rooms, with the draped door by the entrance leading to a restroom walled with mirrors on all six sides. If you've ever been in a room walled with mirrors on all six sides, you'd know that it makes your reflection go off endlessly in all directions. Now imagine that your reflection is taking a shit, is what this restroom is trying to say. There's a scene in *Brüno* where Sacha Baron Cohen just spins his cock around for what feels like thirty minutes, and it spins the way the hands on a clock spin when movies do fast-forwarding bits. I've done that in this restroom, only here, it's endless. The sink in this restroom is made of clay or marble or both and is worth more than my house, I'm sure, and instead of knobs or handles with cursive *Hot* and *Cold* on them to dictate what I'm getting, there are two chubby baby angels, probably Cupids, wearing towels around their waists and holding bows above their heads. I spin one until water starts to come out, and I've got no choice but to wait until it burns me. Rich people are incredibly impractical. It's my favorite room in pool table house.

When I'm not in the endless shitter, I'm hiding behind eight-foot statues of American Indians or sinking into the space between sumo-sized couch cushions. The irony of using a towering American Indian as my shield during Thanksgiving is not lost on me. It's noon, and everybody's hungry because nobody's eaten breakfast in anticipation of a big lunch, including me. I'm convinced that all holiday party hosts in New York state have agreed that the food only comes out once all the guests have collectively forgotten that it's the reason they've all gathered. I'm unsure if this is a New Yorkism, Americanism, or just a Thanksgivingism.

My second favorite room in pool table house and the other place I hide when I'm not squatting in the endless shitter or shadowed behind Squanto is the kitchen, because it's an absolute free-for-all in there. There's six to eight fleet-footed cooks going in like freestyle rappers on whatever they're cheffing up. Things are being wrapped and unwrapped in aluminum foil, and someone is bent and poking the world's longest fork into the oven. These chefs are all half my size, and they scurry like mice leaving trails of whisked air in their wake. Mama Pool Table, the woman of the house, walks around the kitchen like a master chef, dipping a teaspoon into things to check the salt to pepper ratio before barking about paprika in broken, heavily accented Spanish, all the while never looking like she's actually cooking anything herself. It's unclear if she is the decision maker in this kitchen as to *what* will be cooked, but is certainly the judge, jury, and executioner as to *how* it's been cooked. The whole kitchen bathes in the wet oven's yellow-red light, and it's probably fifty degrees hotter here than anywhere else in the house. Whenever one of the chefs notices me hovering like a tall lamp in the corner watching the chaos, and we lock eyes, it's like a mutual cry for help. They stop in their tracks and gaze into me, all red and teary-eyed like the salt-to-pepper ratio is life or death, as if Mama Pool Table has their kids tied up in the basement, threatening *asesinato* if the turkey's dry. I'd like to think that I would offer to help if I could, but I'm acutely aware of my specific talents, which include neither a working knowledge of paprika nor the Spanish language. It's also too hot in there to stay long.

I like to people-watch because I find people both incredibly annoying and incredibly interesting. To complicate, I will say that people who are interestingly annoying I *will* watch, but people who are annoyingly interesting I wholeheartedly refuse. I people watch the same way people watch flies buzz around their legs on the porch, ready to shake them off the second they land. People interacting with each other in a celebratory environment like Thanksgiving are especially easy to watch because I can immediately tell who's actually comfortable talking to who and who's mingling themselves thin. In one corner, you have a dark and scaly *Ooh* hunched over the darker and scalier *Aah*, never once looking at each other as they start conversations with, "so?" These types would sit in one spot and shrug at each other for literal hours if they could, because years of friendship have made them aggressively comfortable with each other. These characters, approachably funny in their predictability, are somehow both raw and overdone. For instance:

"So?"

"*So?*"

"You know, the same."

"Same is good. I wish I were the same."

"Oh yeah, what's changed?"

"Nothing's changed, but nothing's the same neither."

"I get what you mean."

So passive, so easy. It always feels like these kinds of guys are talking through a toothpick on the porch, exuding that warm, rocking chair kind of ease. These guys are nice to spy when they manifest, but are far too regular to be of any real interest, and they aren't all that annoying either. Really, their unassuming friendship is pretty amicable, and seems like something to strive for. It seems right to find someone who gets you to the core level, so much so that they practically *are* you. Then by engaging with that person, you're really just stimulating them into soaking in themselves. The bond is then sealed within both friends, not between them, as if knowing each other makes them more themselves. These guys really have it all, friendship-wise, and it's sickening.

"Yeah. I gotta take a shit."

"I just did in the mirror room. Weird fucking room."

"Crazy weird. I don't get these rich fucks."

"Fun as hell to shit in, though."

"Yeah. I'm going."

Doubtless, the gruesomest joys come from spying on a bit of painful small talk, like when the wives of two blokes who've never met peel off toward the balcony to talk diets (or carbon footprint, we don't forget carbon footprint), and the blokes just slouch deeper into their shoes, stupefied, leaning back against their knees and ogling at lamps in the room's corners. You don't want to get caught in a situation like this without a drink, because a drink is an out. The guy with the drink will inevitably come out on top as the winner of the conversation, because husband-to-husband small talk is all about showing you're more socially adept than the other guy, and husbands with drinks in their hands inevitably come off as more socially adept than husbands without drinks in their hands. The one who wants to leave the most will always talk first.

"Real nice place here," says the guy who's doomed without a drink.

"Gee, thanks. I built the foundation of this friendship with my bare hands." The charisma is fake. It's the drink.

"Say, where'd you get that drink?"

"I, I made this drink."

"I too would like to make myself a drink."

"Well, get to it, peanut. Bar's by the Mohican."

"Where's the bar?"

"Around this hallway, to the left of the Mohican."

"What is a *Mohican*?"

"Son. Go around this hallway and make yourself a drink."

Back at school, I get the sense that to enjoy a college party, most people check their brains at the door and just go dark, total submission to the party atmosphere. I picture them all trying desperately to cram themselves into tiny little sidecars, which, for all intents and purposes, are toy-sized and bright red with itty bitty leather black seats – your classic, idealized sidecar. The sidecar is appealing to the college student because it's essentially responsibility free – nobody blames the sidecar for a crash. But this particular idealized sidecar is simply too small, and the college student is far from a true fit. Still, they try fiendishly to cram themselves in, focusing so intently on how to get into the sidecar that they completely neglect to check what it's attached to. In college, the main car is driven by alcohol, which rolls and riots at high speeds, and doesn't care if that pasty college kid in the sidecar settles in, which they rarely do, perpetually struggling to strap in, to fit. The alcohol just drives without giving the sidecar a single thought, perhaps totally unaware it's even attached to a sidecar, dragging it from one place to the next, while the kid flails and clings on by their ankles exclaiming something about *fraternité*.

On the off chance that anyone ever manages to cram themselves deep enough into the sidecar to consider themselves a true fit, they'll look up and realize that alcohol is their driver, and see the nature of the risk involved in riding. They might consider that after all this effort, it may have been an even more valuable use of their time to take some responsibility and get behind the wheel of the main car, instead of fighting to fit into the sidecar. I digress.

In a sense, this sidecar phenomenon persists for the same reasons that people with drinks in their hands seem more socially adept than people without drinks in their hands. But at holiday parties, the reckless driver of the main car is not alcohol, but small talk, and the people trying to fit in are older, larger, and less flexible. That guy with the drink is clinical sidecar who's managed to fake it all day as a driver. Seems like a torrential douche. I hope he doesn't ask me who's kid I am.

"Hey kid. You look like you've been sitting here watching people. You bored?"

"I go to Fordham University in the City. I'm majoring in Biomedical Engineering with a concentration on annulation. I am in my Junior year."

"Got that one on repeat, huh? I remember when I was your age. All these random oldies asking me what I wanted to do with my days. Yikes. Here, 'ave some of this drink."

"College has made me a nihilist. I am also a semi-alcoholic. I am also a semi-vegetarian with premonitions of gluten-free."

"Jesus, kid. They got you wound tighter than a fat bitch wedgie. Loosen your gears, brother. You smoke?"

"I am a recovering marijuana dependent. Tobacco is a class one carcinogen. I don't smoke."

"Alright kid. You seriously need to wake up. You know what you sound like?"

I am pretty sure I know what he thinks I sound like, and it's exactly what I want him to think. I loathe small talk about my university habits, but what I loathe even more are torrential douchebags, and this particular torrential douchebag is the kind of person who's double your age when the 'rents are around but tries to be "hip" when you're alone with them. Also, unlike my university colleagues, I loathe people who try to scale social barriers by asking if they can drug me. Alright, I'm ready. Tell me what I know you think I sound like.

"You sound like a robot."

" "
"..."

"…"

"…"

"You know that?"

"Robots sound like robots. What else?"

"What else is, you're not a robot, kid. You're a kid."

"I am the CS-5000, "Home For The Holidays" Edition. Manufactured by SYK Robotics in Santa Clarita, California, 2018. Would you like me to laugh at your next joke?"

"Yeah, laugh at everything I say from now on. I want to see you play this out."

"HaHaHa."

"You look pretty real for a bot, kid. Where are the buttons and lights and whatnot?"

"HaHaHa. I have been designed to mimic natural life in every way, in both appearance and behavior. More specifically, I was designed to mimic Kyle Johns, son of Louis and Jane Johns, from Lancaster, New York. My purpose is to fill the place of the real Kyle Johns, who is with his girlfriend's family this Thanksgiving."

"And why the hell are you telling me you're a robot if you are one? Doesn't that go against your programming or something?"

"HaHaHa. Good question. I have been designed to explain my design to those who notice the indescribable differences between myself and a human. This is to avoid the misconception that the real Kyle Johns is in any way responsible for my mistakes."

"And they programmed you to tell me you have a weed problem?"

"HaHaHa. I was programmed not to question my creators."

"Gotcha. Alright. I'm over it, kid. Turn off."

"HaHaHa. I was designed to comply only with my parents' orders."

"Alright, you win. Bye, kid."

"HaHaHa. Bye, douchebag."

I tried to tweak and rumble as a real machine would when it's splashed with liquid, but I think it came off as a bit stale. There weren't any sparks flying around either. It took a small fleet of hungry old blokes to pull the torrential douche off me, after the crash of his whiskey glass brought us to the room's attention. I sort of just laid limp and flexed real hard as they handled him, seeing as the gag was my only claim to victory in this bit of small talk. Nobody blamed me when the whole thing was over, except probably the torrential douche, who was so blushed and heated when they pulled him off me that he ditched the place before even giving thanks. The American Indian in the corner was proud of me for sticking to the gag. I could tell by his cool smile and downward nod. After that, I went back to the endless shitter and swung my dick around 'til dinner.

7

Heads, Shoulders, Knees, Toes

HEADS

How far could you walk with your eyes closed? I can't go far. The first few seconds are easy, but it becomes more and more unnerving the longer I go. It's not like anything's going to pop out in front of me, I make sure of that before I begin the process. Maybe I'm a control freak, but the fear of not knowing exactly what's happening in front of me at all times is overwhelming enough that more than five seconds of darkness is frightening. Don't get me wrong. I'm not afraid of darkness; I do sleep once a day, after all. It's the movement, forward, of course. I couldn't imagine walking backward with my eyes closed; that causes instability within me that can't be defeated by practice. I try to walk with my eyes closed every day, and I've never been able to keep them shut for longer than about four seconds. Four seconds, my maximum capacity for losing control. I don't fear anything but this instability; I know this. Shit, maybe I'll trip. Maybe I'll step on a butterfly. Maybe the love of my life will pass me by. But all I'll miss is four seconds worth. Come to think of it, that's not too bad, right?

But fuck. Why am I walking with my eyes closed in the first place?

SHOULDERS

Some fucker once said that Atlas shrugged. What does that even mean? Fuck you, Ayn Rand. Fuck your face. Of course he shrugged. He was carrying the weight of the world on his shoulders, you inconsiderate fuck. He probably was shrugging not because the world was heavy, but because he was so sick of eternally having to carry around a bunch of fuckers like you on his shoulders. But hey, that curse was eternal so, *shrug*, what's a guy gonna do?

KNEES

I can't remember the last time I went out of my way to wash my knees or below. But like, the body wash from my torso always drips down to my legs anyway, kind of glazing over my knee skin before being violently washed away, so it's not like they go completely neglected. Granted, this is a phenomenon that goes totally unnoticed to me as I bury inexplicably-blue Old Spice shampoo into the depths of my scalp with my eyes closed, shouting the opening to Ultralight Beams at my clearly moved showerhead.

TOES

My toenails are too long, but they're also a part of me I genuinely don't care about. To expand, I actually don't think about my feet like ever during the day. I cover them in dirty rags with a big hole at the top and then hide them in somewhat protective layers of fabric. Isn't that kind of fucked? My feet are usually the only connection between me and the ground, a perfectly angled body part that balances my pinned structure with the perpendicular ground below me. Feet are dope, they literally keep us grounded. Toes are fucking pointless, though. Our feet would work just fine without them. But seriously, flip-flops are dope, so I guess toes can stay.

8

Excerpts from "Waves"

another novel I will never finish

Mutability

33° 28'15"N 117° 43' 06"W
*Breakers Isle, Dana Point, CA 92692, a stone's throw from the
Pacific Ocean*

Ever since his wife Natalia was stolen from reality, her mind going like a sand-castle at high tide, he'd given up all hope of completing his magnum opus novel. How could he, when each day all his energies are devoted to reminding the greatest woman he knows that she's his? The absence of her love's hold stealing with it the comfort of knowing that he's hers? He bathes her, feeds her, reads her passages of poetry she once wrote. His life's thrust now is to give the one he loves all she could never return, shackled by a commitment he'd made long ago, a commitment he keeps long past the time she forgot what her own commitments were. If marriage is a tug-of-war between partners, Natalia's husband Gad has spent the last seven years pulling an endless rope without resistance, piling it up in layers behind him, letting it grow so tall he's begun to disappear into its shadow.

Of course, the comfort-of-knowing surpasses any physical comfort. Not even his terrace view of the monumentally lovely Dana Point does the trick, his aged skull hardening to physical pleasure of any kind that isn't whitewashed with guilt that it's a pleasure his wife can't share. Often he sets her on the terrace with him at sunset, just to watch her eyes as they reflect the sky's gloss of reds and yellows, only to find nothing in them but a thick dusk over an ocean of blues. He wonders if each day to her he is something new, a different shade of the same protective color, providing for her in ways she could never pin down... or is he a developing picture of a memory once held dear, something warm?

The idea is a hopeful one, but unrealistic to the intuitive mind. Intuitive, perceptive, intelligent, he is all the above – and always has been – but is also nothing more than human, susceptible to attaching himself to any glimmer of hope, an attachment that can't be reasoned through by even the most logical mind. The grip of an ideology buried deep in his core, unable to be removed or detached, guides him toward irrational self-healing. The replenishing wave of hopefulness in the face of the impossible storm, driven by a faint and distant light, like the vignetted image of a proud mother telling you to Keep Going, Going, Going toward a light that has weathered the same impossible storm to reach you... but the back of your mind stuck wondering what if... what if you weather the storm only to find upon passing it by that the light was imagined, and you are forced to face your own delusions? Would the journey have been for nothing?

"It's about the journey, not the destination," Gad remembers being reassured by his mother as a boy, a statement he doubled-back on for his own daughter years ago. For Gad, the hopeful light isn't even imagined, it's real, and it comes each morning in the form of whispered dreams from his half-woken wife. He notes them, but without the dream's context, they're meaningless. Gad considers context now, as he sits cross-legged on his terrace facing the slow-burning dawn, still time before he should return to bed to catch his wife's first words of the day and scribble them down in his pocketbook.

Seagulls hang low and sing an empty song to the beach. The houses to his left and right have terraces exactly like his, although no people are on them. Gad's cell phone rings to his left.

"Hello?"

A seagull lets loose another empty bellow of sound, mimicked with insensitive loudness by a surfer on the water. It may or may not have just started to rain. The clouds look placed.

"Heeellooooo?"

Natalia wakes earlier than usual to an empty room and whispers into her pillow. Gad hangs up the phone, feeling robbed of audible stimulation. He goes inside and turns on the living room TV. Underneath the terraces' maple floorboards, a cockroach tips over onto its back.

"...op story today is Syd Soul, A-list hip hop star and notorious..." the early morning anchorman makes air quotes as he says this... "'Free Thinker'... is entering his seventh day as a patient at Pale Hollow Psychiatric Hospital, where his family committed him after reportedly showing..." no air quotes here... "Suicidal tendencies.... There have been no reports from the hospital about Soul's recovery other than that he is currently receiving treatment, release date unknown. Soul has *made waves recently following a series of viral video posts where he passionately verbalized his views about various social and political issues, including but not limited to: civil rights advances for gays and African-Californians, concerns with the California Department of Education, and anger with the Silicon Valley tech and data company YourWeb. Some believe that Soul's antics are no more than an eccentric marketing scheme for his new album PERCOCEPTION."*

Gad leaves the TV to continue spewing rudely as a round man with a handlebar mustache dubbed "Psychiatric Expert" gets half the screen's attention. Gad's barefoot steps toward the bedroom shoot a vacant echo across the marble floor tiles. In their bedroom, Natalia reacquaints herself with the inside of her body. The portrait of her husband and her daughter with their arms around her is aptly placed on the bedside table for just this kind of situation, so she's only shocked, not frightened, when Gad steps through the door.

"Good morning, love," Gad says. Natalia nods her head but doesn't, more of a dumbfounded twitch.

"Any dreams tonight?"

Her eyes cross the way anyone's do when looking at a thing they can't understand. She's heard the words before, and can sense that maybe once she would have reacted to them, but now her comprehension is left hidden under her tongue. She can only hum.

Gad crosses the bed and kisses his wife on the shoulder, a movement she stares at in awe. He looks into her pale brown eyes but sees no light inside them, only remnants of a reflection from the dim light in his own. Hope's grip on him has become something he feels daily. No longer the subterranean propellor of his morality and goodwill, it's now the lighthouse to his stranded sea traveler, promising some sort of relief if only he can reach it. But with that promise a hint that relief, like passive comfort, makes only for an empty existence. He wonders if Natalia sees the emptiness in his eyes, or sees anything at all, or if they reflect a different moral absolute within her own. She owes him nothing. He owes her less.

"Suicidal Tendencies" is what the anchorman had said the man had. A tendency, like one's tendency to prefer chocolate to vanilla, or to interrupt people in conversation. An inclination toward a particular characteristic or behavior – a tendency to want to die. People often make habits of tendencies, but death can never become habitual. No one can die both today and tomorrow. There is no *tendency to die*. Only a tendency to *want* to die. A preference of death over life. Habitual dying seems a godly form of escape from a life like his, but habitual *wanting* is a special kind of hell.

Gad's life has become habitually dull, characterized by a tendency to tend to his wife, herself dead in every realm not physical. But what of his daughter? The guilt of abandoning her would ride him until his lighthouse is reached, and only then might it transform into something else. But what? He's gone through this all before.

His daughter's light is the only one he can still sense the warmth of, still truly believes can take pleasure from shining on him. But ever since she moved away, leaving him alone to be mocked by the gulls, his guilt about possibly leaving her has started to vanish like a light behind settling fog. But this guilt is consoled only fleetingly, the consolation of his daughter's abandonment obscured by an understanding that she's off educating the new world, a better world, one perhaps worth living in. Could he justify abandoning a girl he brought up to believe in something more? Could he choose death knowing full well that his daughter's total will is being put toward choosing life? One moment he feels the guilt of abandonment dissolve in the blank and tragic eyes of a loved soul lost. The next it returns, and with it a glimmer of hope, hope he knows he himself may never touch again, but whose radiant warmth just might be enough.

_o__ _ ___ o_ ____ ____

It's the whiteness of the whole place that's why it's so scary. A kind of whiteness that glares over itself like it's both donut and display case, you the doughboy trouser-clad adolescent with a rainbow windmill cap, eyes wide over a nose pressed warmly into the sweatless glass, feeling your ignorant remorseless awe for some flakey pink-and-white sprinkle-covered drizzle-of-shit that's just too good to be true, and it is, because you're step-maw is pulling you by the collar away to the car and you're dragging your feet and cringing through the veins in your forehead over chocolate ganache and a glass of chilled milk as you pass, and you feel some type of hushed glare glaze over the disappearing sprinkle, donut, glass case now fading like a rapid zoom that's always two thumbs out of reach, but you don't really see the glare as much as sense it by accident, just a bi-product, the chance of your line of sight crossing it and it's suddenly there, the reflection both within and without the display case that isn't anything more than a freckle of dust in your eye or the sound of your step-maw's flat toned steps, something you feel the pressure of without really gestating, without letting it hone you, without becoming possessed. Soon the display case fades into the unintelligible whiteness of your past with the rest of the donuts you almost stuffed and the women who too were always a thumb or a fist or a pointer's reach away but you remember, though unsure if it's the initial experience you're remembering or if you're just remembering the last time you remembered, infinitely cropping your most visceral moments into stretched toffee semblances of themselves, but the roof of your mouth still moistens and your tongue still quivers when you pass a glass display case because your weakness stays with you, the whiteness of your best dreams still half the strobe in your worst nightmares, leading you or even gliding alongside, though never falling behind. The whiteness is worst when it jumps out at you like a deer on a midnight country drive, or a deerlike face poking a claw through the window in the front door to serve you, and it's just there, one moment it wasn't, but now it's right there and you're facing it, and you're reminded of how it felt that last time you remembered it and it hurts – like the whiteness of a dentist's gloved wrist as you lay prone on the table and his glove gives your molars a rubbery rub, and his collar is white, and his shirt and his pants are too and the chair that he sits on is a sort of sandy off white and the repurposable murder weapon that towers over you and flashes a wide white light into your eyes is matte white, and his assistant is white in white stockings and white shoes with white laces and the floor is white but checkered with thin lines of a grayish off-white that make you and the dentist and the dentist's assistant plotted points on the floor grid, nobody rising or running because of the special showmanship of dentistry, the medical interpretive dance that freezes all viewers in white place. But the most suffocating whiteness comes when you learn that of course you're all fine and your crown is still in place, and the cavity repair is on track, and all that anxiety over the whiteness of the room and the possibility of fading into the blur of it all was all aimless, though you're never quite sure if the doctor is delivering trustworthy news because of his sideways look, his red moustache but blond hair, and the way he calls your step-maw *Gwendolyn.*

Pale Hollow Psychiatric Hospital is a massive cylindrical building of cream-white with eight floors above ground and two below. It is built atop a hill once part of Chino

Hills State Park. The hill was sold along with a small flat area of land for parking to Dr. Maxim Panko at $1.3 million when Chino Hills started getting the heat-milk real bad and needed some fast cash to invest in water treatment (even though nobody went to CHSP anymore anyway). So Panko bought the hill and built roads up to Carbon Canyon and Butterfield Ranch and Yorba Linda Blvd., and the whole restructuring and construction of PHPH took around seven years and cost Panko no less than an arm and a leg.

Panko made it big in 2048 after patenting the Guided Thoughts™ ear-implant for the hopelessly mentally ill, which pretty much does exactly what it sounds like. The tech works by monitoring a patient's brain synapses 24/7, and whenever a thought deemed "counter-productive" starts to coast through one's neurotransmitters, the implant intervenes and stops it, puts a wall around the thought, and doesn't let it disturb the healing brain. The thought doesn't just go away because the implant is a non-eradicant, meaning it can trap a bad thought but can't kill it, so when a thought gets trapped by Guided Thoughts, the patient might feel a slight itch on the side of their nose or an urge to wiggle their chin, which everyone agrees is worth the upside. Side effects were much worse during trial periods; some rats and guinea pigs turned crispy like baked potatoes or had teeth shoot out as their heads exploded into the glass. Moreover, the problem with animal testing was that there was no way to know if a bad thought for a human was also a bad thought for an animal, so showing pictures of dead rats and moldy cheese on an LED screen in front of the glass cage while playing a high pitched screech noise and watching the implant guide the feral impulse was in itself counter-productive, as even once they'd made tweaks so the implant would stop cooking rats, there was no way to tell if the animals non-reaction was a success for the implant or a misunderstanding of what really makes rats squirm. So this problem cost Panko's team months of budgeted time before they decided they had to have human trials, and because some homeless people will do a lot for a roof, buck, and some warm meals, Panko had assembled a team of 10 schizoid or severely depressed folk within a week and went to work. Because humans know what other humans don't like and because it's easy to ask another human what they don't like, it was relatively simple to find out what would trigger a negative thought, and once they had done that, it was just a matter of letting the implant do its thing. Of course, there were failures, but by this time, they had moved past the early stage kinks and weren't frying people or yanking out their canines, so the worst of the early round human side effects were sleepless nights, loss of appetite, and a 24-hour strong aversion to bright lights. Over the course of the next 22 months, Panko, his wife Louellen, and their team of research assistants had developed a product that gave the schizoid, the severely depressed, the aggressively anxious, or even the perennially pessimistic a new lease on life (and also moved Panko up a handful of tax brackets). But since completing his life's work left Panko with that cliché reach-the-top-and-realize-success-isn't-everything type sadness, he decided to open a recovery center for the extremely wealthy or high-profile so he could keep busy.

A sort of Reaganomic approach to mental health treatment, Panko preaches through books, book tours, paid speaking events and sometimes casual conversation that the societal mental health problem is really as simple as a system of social pressures following the same hierarchy as race relations or economic ills, and that curing the leaders of society, whether they be government officials, corporate heads or big name celebs will trickle down and help out the depressed average-joe. The basis for this theory is that happier and healthier leaders treat their workers and populace better, more or less following the theoretical lines of Ronald Reagan's supply-side economics of the 1980s, which Panko's folks, one a shipping magnate and the other an investment and loan titan, had loved so much.

So here is his place, Pale Hollow Psychiatric Hospital in Chino Hills State Park. It's a good place. It does its job, if its job is to change people's minds. Some say that the mind is an indestructible force; Panko and the folks at PHPH disagree. Here, the mind is a canvas for Panko to develop the future, and canvases are necessarily blank. If Panko were in the business of healing, he'd be a doctor. Doctors and psychiatrists are different. Panko does not want to heal, he wants to fix, to adjust. A body does not revolve into PHPH's conditioned lobby with bruises, scrapes, blood gushing from the orifices. A body falls into the open arms of Panko and his team and becomes just that – a body – for as long as it takes to change the mind. The weight leaves the legs, and the PHPH staff takes on the body's full burden. Empty shells walk the halls of PHPH with that same look the mentally ill carry as they scrape socked soles against the shadowless hallways of TV's dreariest mental hospitals. This is not a drill, this is full body dismissal. Check your organs at the door and remember that so long as time is spent in PHPH, the brain is the main course, and if Panko could cut off heads, adjust their perception and screw them back on, he would. He may soon invest in platinum trays to return them to their keepers in fashion.

"Welcome to Pale Hollow, Mr. Soul. Please follow me to your room."

Syd Soul is a seriously important person. A guy of great influence, who sets trends for people he's never met, and who people who don't even follow trends still have to sometimes think about because of his effect on the people they know. In many, he inspires jealousy, which is a feeling that one wouldn't typically find inspirational, but it has shades, and the shade Soul brings out of those he influences is inspirational. They hate him because they want to be him, and in working toward doing so, they have one of two choices: change how they feel about him or learn to hate themselves. It's no guess which choice most make.

He's sitting in a wheelchair he doesn't really need, being rolled through the dreadfully white PHPH first-floor lobby by a person who knows who they're rolling. Soul and his roller don't speak at all, don't even exchange pleasantries, not even when the elevator door takes too long to shut and they both notice, and both wait, expecting the other to push that sideways inward facing carrot close door button that every elevator has. Syd doesn't do it because he's in a wheelchair, and duh, it's absolutely *not* his job to make that sort of thing happen, *especially* here and now, and his roller (who shall remain nameless) doesn't do it because they (also genderless) are totally shellshocked and nervous about being the person who's supposed to make sure that *the* Syd Soul – pop-culture and music icon turned fashion mogul turned social disrupter (though the signs were always there) who absolutely dominates Grammys, who pretty much gets harassed for his John Hancock in any sullen corner of this green Earth, who's wife is not only remarkably recognizable and attractive but who in her own right also makes sullen corners writhe with envy, who single-handedly has initiated and made popular his strong doubts of not one but *four* sitting U.S. Presidents, who's been begged by both Oprah and Ken Burns to himself run for our land's highest office and who's said no, sincerely, to even the *idea* of a Presidential run, or to ever being subjected to act in any way by and for the will of any person that does not live wholly within his own skull, the very same skull which has since gone publicly defect and landed him where he is now, in this wheeled chair which they roll – doesn't get worked up. Though the door closes itself not long after.

Waiting in a nondescript office for his doctor, Syd stares at the right wall. Now more of a watcher, his once roller sits in the corner behind him. Footsteps precede a voice which precedes a woman, tall and stiff.

"Thank you, nurse, that's all."

The watcher leaves the room, and the Dr. takes a seat. Quite literally "takes", she doesn't sit down as much as snatch the chair, as if racing to it. She uncaps a red pen and holds it in her left hand, a yellow legal pad already face-up on her desk. She scribbles to dislodge dry ink, then looks up at Syd, who's still looking at the wall.

"Pale Hollow. You're familiar with her work?"

"..."

"She was an actress in the late fifties. Stunning. Hopelessly true in any role. That picture you're staring so intently at was taken here, in the greenhouse. She came here in sixty-four when she was just thirty-three years old. You're also thirty-three years old, aren't you, Syd?"

"..."

"You're never too old. Our programs are proven for all ages. Pale was our first patient before both your and my time. Maxim was greatly dedicated to her cause. Wanted desperately for her to leave this place and return to the stage. It's all fable now. His love for her and divorce from Louellen, renaming the hospital after her tragic death."

"Death?"

"Yes, Pale died in a car crash a week after her release. Tragic. A wondrous actress, marvelous really. She's survived by her work."

"..."

"..."

"..."

"Maxim is desperate to see you. Dreadfully excited you've decided to join us. We're all incredibly charmed by your music."

"..."

"And your art. Clothing. And influence."

"..."

"I'll get to it then. You're here for four weeks, depending. The first week will be basic introductions, pleasantries, baths in the hot springs. The next week we'll begin the process of understanding, both within and without, and get a firm grip on the why and how of your visit. In the third week, we will begin implementing Guided Thoughts, working out kinks, etc. In the last week, you'll tell us what you've learned."

"It won't take me a week to introduce myself. Can't we get that out of the way right here and now?"

"We could, but that isn't how we typically do things here. Are you already in a hurry to leave?"

"I just don't see why any of this is necessary."

"Your family seems to think it is."

"My family doesn't know me. They were fine when all I did was play the part they wanted me to play. The day I decided to be my own person, they didn't know what to do. That's why they sent me here. Me being here says more about them than it does about me."

"It says a bit about both. But a bit is not enough. We need to know you, all of you, the part you played and the person you are. Otherwise, we're just shooting from the hip."

"What I'm saying is I don't belong here."

"Then what's the harm in staying a while to let us figure that out for ourselves?"

"..."

"Syd. Are you religious?"

"I'm spiritual."

"What's the difference?"

"I don't need a church to tell me what to listen to. I hear God on my own."

"Are you afraid of God?"

"God doesn't want me to fear Him. He just wants to talk."

"And when you two talk, does God tell you that you've got it all figured out?"

"He doesn't talk with words we can understand. God speaks his own language."

"Can you understand what He says?"

"Sometimes."

"And other times?"

"No."

"Wouldn't you like to know what He's saying? Not just some of the time, but every time?"

"Of course."

"Then take his silence as a sign. Maybe you're here for a reason."

"Maybe I'm supposed to leave."

"Maybe you are. Listen, I have no dog in this fight. If you think you should leave, I can't legally stop you. I'm not going to tell you that four weeks in our facility will solve all your problems, but there's a nonzero chance that it might. If you want to hear God, really hear him, why shun the people who're dedicated to helping you do that?"

"You sound like my step-maw when she'd drop me off at Sunday school."

"Really. And what would they teach you at Sunday school?"

"Nothing. I ditched every week to drum buckets outside the Metro."

"Do you ever feel like maybe you missed out?"

"On what?"

"On what they had to teach you. The wisdom they wanted to share."

"I learned everything I needed to from those buckets."

"Then why are you here?"

"Because nobody believes me when I say I'm alright."

"Do you fully believe yourself?"

"I don't know."

"Then give us a shot. In return, I'll make you a promise."

"..."

"I promise to get you closer to that answer."

"What if that doesn't work?"

"Then you can leave here totally sure that you really are alright. That everyone was wrong – your stepmother, your wife, your Sunday school teachers, me. Nobody understood you, and you were right. Because sitting across from you now, I can tell you still aren't sure."

"How?"

"Because you haven't looked away from that portrait on the wall since you got in."

"It's a beautiful picture."

"Of a woman who reminds me a lot of you. A woman who thought that everything was alright and that the world outside was evil and wrong. I see you in her."

"And what's the problem with that?"

"No problem at all. But she wasn't sure either, and a week after we let her go, she died for it."

"..."

"I don't want that for you, Syd. Nobody does. I pray that you're right, that the only thing you need is a bucket to drum on. But with her, with Pale Hallow, it didn't take long to learn that the bucket was flipped the whole time. She was inside-out, convinced she was on the right side of her world. Give us, and yourself, a few weeks to know for sure that you're different. What could go wrong?"

"..."

"..."

"The bucket was flipped."

"And her head was inside it."

"I wonder what that sounds like."

"Me too. All I know is, it makes it damn hard to drum."

9

Three, And A Dog

Roger's in the bathroom. Roger might burn his lip on that tea, Carol says to Shane. Roger and Carol are together but not in love, though they sometimes tell each other they are, but Carol still tells herself that he said it first, and she said it more as a reaction to him saying it than a choice to say it herself. She wouldn't have said it first, but she felt that to keep things flowing, it was best to say it. Shane tells Carol that he'll put five dollars down that Roger does burn his lip, and Carol won't take that bet. Shane picks lint off his tweed jacket and flicks it onto the Persian rug under the table, which is made of hardwood. In the room's corner, "When Harry Met Sally" plays on the 44-inch LG TV, which Roger and Carol got at Best Buy three Black Fridays ago at forty percent off, and nobody watches.

Roger comes back to the dining room. Roger asks Shane what brings him to town. Shane cups his hands over the steam from his hot cup of earl grey and says "work." Carol taps her acrylic nails on the table in sets of three – ring finger, middle finger, pointer – pausing briefly between sets. Her eyes fall onto the empty napkin holder at the table's center, and she leaves them there, exhaling deeply. Roger remarks on the funny way that Kirby, his and Carol's puppy pug, is curled up asleep on the floor next to the fridge. Carol looks at Shane, who smiles. Carol says that Kirby has been super tired lately, always asleep or half asleep, and she thinks she or Roger should take him to the vet. Shane loses his smile, gets out of his chair, and walks over to Kirby. He kneels down and pets his slick, gray-black fur. Do dogs have fur, or is it hair? Shane asks, half-joking. Roger laughs much more than he should. Carol smiles too. Carol says fur. Roger says some have fur and others have hair. Carol adds that others are bald. They all laugh again, and When Harry Met Sally goes to commercial.

Carol asks Shane if a straw has one hole or two. He says one. Roger, who wasn't asked, says two. Carol tells Roger that Shane is right, it's one deep hole, and Roger makes a face. Shane asks Roger if a taco is a sandwich, and Roger corrects him to say that the question really is if hot dogs are sandwiches, not tacos. Carol says they're both wrong, and the question is a fallacy because a hot dog is actually a taco. They all laugh again, and Kirby perks up his head like he wants in on the fun. They laugh some more.

Roger asks Carol when she got so witty, and moves for his tea. Shane sees him move for it and motions with his head for Carol to look. They watch him put it to his lip, which gets burned by the tea. Roger makes a show of having a burnt lip, and Carol looks at Shane and says she called it. Shane laughs, Kirby gets up, and Roger looks at Shane. Roger starts to laugh and spills a little tea on the floor. Kirby goes to it and laps up the tea, not bothered by the heat. Shane is still laughing, and now Carol laughs too.

Roger, Shane, and Carol are spending the night together at Roger and Carol's studio apartment in Brooklyn, which is too small for the price. It's homey, and Roger and Carol will probably stay there for one more year before Carol gets pregnant and they decide to get a more spacious place. Roger and Carol are not in love, and actually Roger thinks that Carol and Shane might be sleeping together. He's been up and down about mentioning his worry to Carol, but is still waiting for the right time. Shane's arrival was a bit of a surprise, but he's nice enough to have around, and Roger thinks maybe it's alright if he *is* sleeping with Carol. After all, they're good fun to hang out with, and he doesn't want to throw a wrench into things. The truth is, Shane and Carol *are* sleeping together, but they both like Roger, too. They all feel a little bit bad about the state of everything, but tonight everyone's alright with hot tea and a laugh.

10

A Matter of Belief

Speaking to Alan, who's hunched over towers of leaflets on the opposite side of the desk, would be easier if Charles turned and faced him, but instead Charles chooses to face the wall-sized window and speak into the glass. He does this not only because it is less bothersome than directing his words at a person who is clearly not listening, but because he feels it adds a lofty destructiveness to each word, like he's dropping bombs on the sprawling city. He speaks:

"Everyone I know wishes only to take from me. There's no more compassion, no more respect; they don't even fake it anymore. Ever since the beginning, I've given them so much, but the giving just led to more taking. What will be left of me once they've taken it all?"

Alan licks both thumbs as he matches court orders, subpoenas, and newspaper clippings to their corresponding company files. He deals documents like they're high stakes poker hands into parallel piles on the great desk, almost completely without thought, registering only bits of what

Charles is saying, aware that his work is more likely to save them than anything Charles could say.

Alan: "There's still hope yet. To our knowledge, the company isn't against you – Lewis and Rothman both expressed support on the record in *the Journal,* which should keep the dogs off for at least a few more days. Bearbull has been quoted separately by journalists at *the Daily* and *the Times* in the last week, which tells me that he hasn't got enough on you to keep busy. Once he disappears for a while, we'll know he's working up a case, and anyway, we've still got months until trial. Until then, there's nothing left for him, or anyone, to take, Charles. It's up to you to set the tone."

Charles has always preferred hard things that seem impossible to escape. Like a rat stuck in a corner, trouble is the state in which he thinks most clearly. The problem with his current position is that there is very little thinking to be done, very few cards unturned, no hands left to play. He lies at the will of a praise-seeking district attorney, while being cornered by a fanged soon-to-be ex-wife and a board of shadow-lurking directors who smell blood. It seems to Charles that all the individuals who once held seats at the table in his mind's very own Last Supper were now simply waiting for the charges to come in from D.A. Bearbull, knives gripped and glands salivating at the thought of cutting themselves a piece of his pie. The cloudless New York spring afternoon looks deceptively warm from Charles' penthouse window. "What of my wife?"

"Oh... *Clarissa* has been making the tabloid rounds, trying to cause a stir with that vampire lawyer of hers. She's screaming into the void, Charles, don't let her noises keep you up."

Her name had become a source of searing pain for Charles. She held and exercised her absolute advantage over him in a way his previous ex-wives never could. His last two divorces were more bombastic and his ex-wives more outrageous in their fury, but those dealings were nowhere as spiritually taxing as this one. She had a way of probing him, molding his image of her from a distance, her hold over him pressing harder on his mind than the D.A.'s wish to put him behind bars, or the board hovering above his head like a thundercloud. She was all they could hope to be and worse, and he was trapped in her prison long before the others caught wind.

The glass fogs incrementally as Charles speaks. "When I first came here, I only wanted to be seen as equal, as anything but *less than*. It took me decades to climb the ladder, but I did it, not because I had to, but because it was how things moved. I made enemies along the way, but who wouldn't in my position? I was a magnet for takers. Everyone wanted a piece of me until I couldn't get away. I got locked in at the top too old, and I couldn't retire, couldn't leave the company I had worked so hard to build. But with the power came the stresses, and with the stresses came the pain. The pain of giving."

Alan scribbles *The Pain of Giving* on the left margin of what seems a particularly dense court order. "Sounds like you just named your memoir!"

The sun is immensely bright but gives off little heat, situated frighteningly low above the rusted black and white city structures, cutting especially crisp into Charles' penthouse window and casting his tiresome shadow over Alan, who, unfortunately for Charles, is exponentially less productive in low light.

It's common street knowledge that magazines burn better than newspapers, because of their thickness and density, when all you're after is a long slow burn. This is why stacks of rolled up *Business Week* and *Forbes* rest charred at the bottom of the two black metal bins in Rico's lot, because they burn slower than the *Times* in the face of the bone-chilling New York night.

Rico, Tom, and E.Z. are invisible to passers-by as they meld into their belongings, the way tenured homeless sometimes do. A motley crew of plastic bags, earth-toned glass bottles, and material – stacks and stacks of material – make ant hills that surround the three compadres whose state is something like half-sleep. Two material-loaded shopping carts encase the boys on both sides like endzones, untied but somehow not rolling down the driveway at the top of which they're situated. The day is bright but not warm, and the wind swirls, so Rico's leaves spin in little grounded tornadoes around his lot.

Make no mistake, these *are* Rico's leaves, his carts, his stacks of material. Everything in the lot is Rico's because this is Rico's lot. Tom and E.Z. are friendly but dispensable, and are keen not to fuck with Rico or his lot, because as long as they remain in his good graces, the material, the carts, and the whole great bounty of Rico's lot is theirs too. In this way, Rico is a gracious god. So when E.Z. leaves each afternoon to collect *Business Week* and *Forbes*, he does so with pride, knowing that this is his role for the betterment of the collective, and he works to bring home more fuel for the fire each day. That's how E.Z. sees Rico's lot: home. If he wants to keep it that way, he needs to produce.

Tom is less financially obligated to Rico, because they're bound as holdovers from an earlier lot where they served Desmond, a god less gracious than Rico, as the shareholders who retrieved the daily magazines. But after Desmond got nasty-wrecked by a motorcycle last winter, his lot went hayloose when all five remaining tenants fought tooth and nail for the treasures he left behind. Colette took Bernardo's guts out with a straw-pipe over a box of soft cotton, and

GINSBERG

Munia L. got dematerialized by the fuzz running through Hell's Kitchen with a bag of needleless syringes. Once Tom and Rico teamed up and overpowered Collette, they were quick to divvy up the remaining loot and pack for greener pastures. Tom didn't mind ceding authority over the new lot to Rico, who was more assertive than he and always seemed to have a plan. Since then, they've developed a bond where few things are said but much is understood, and lay half-sleep amongst their belongings most days.

Rico isn't specific about his feelings that everything (even the air) in his lot belongs to him. He has a general conception of what that really means for him and his compadres but feels that as long as they seem to abide by it, it need not be mentioned. If he needed to, he would tell them that this was his lot because he claimed it, and if somebody else wanted it, they'd have to take it from him. Luckily for Rico, his lot is largely uninteresting to passers-by and remains tentatively off the general homeless radar, leading him, Tom, and the newly acquired E.Z. to live a rather laissez-faire lifestyle. Rico trusts Tom and relies on E.Z., but largely avoids interfering with either of them as they do to him. The lot is a self-stabilizing enterprise, and its benefits – security, warmth, reliability – are allocated equally to all parties involved.

Diagonally across from Rico's lot is a small corner park, the physical and symbolic heart of which is a tall, unnaturally black marble statue resting atop a naturally white marble plinth which reads, *Adam Smith 1723 – 1790, The Father of Economics*. E.Z. passes the statue on his afternoon magazine hunts each day, and has often considered that it seemed to him that all "fathers" of anything important had ubiquitously regular names: *John Adams, Steve Jobs, Henry Ford*. Adam Smith was no different, and led E.Z. to think that maybe the people with the most generic names felt like they had to make up for it somehow, release themselves of the shackles of regularity, and literally "make a name for themselves."

E.Z. considers a concept along these lines semi-regularly on his way to and fro the poorly guarded newsstands and corner stores he cops magazines from, but never in those exact terms, because like Rico, E.Z. isn't very articulate. However, although homeless and oftentimes mindless, E.Z. is far from brainless. Copping mags in large quantities isn't exactly slight work, as Rico and Tom could attest. It requires stealth, reckless ambition, and a blanket disregard for the possibility of failure. E.Z. is a natural, and as such, hoists glorious cartons full of *BusinessWeek* and *Forbes* past the Smith statue each day. He relishes his work defying Smith's legacy as a capitalistic icon, as if the fatherly marble statue couldn't bear to watch the little homeless guy get his. More than the statue, it was the white marble plinth that raised it that prodded at E.Z.'s perennially nagged conscience. A statue wasn't enough for the father of greed? His overbearing stature had to be firmly rooted in the ground, his ideology planted in the streets? E.Z., who'd dropped out of high school and run away from home, was never taught that Smith was, in fact, the pioneer theorist on morality's role in economics, and preached that economies could be both successful and good. In light of this not knowing, E.Z.'s displeasure with the towering figure's presence made his smile wider and more carnivorous each day, as his gaze pierced straight through the legacy of the statue, all the while hoisting his cartons so high. While E.Z. was indebted to Rico and worked each day to secure his place with him, his will to cop 'zines came from a different place, a mental battle with the father of everything he didn't have.

Charles is not a bad man, the way all rich old mysterious men who stare solemnly from penthouse windows are predictably bad. He draws from an adolescence of no wealth, and through dedication and excellence, rose like sewer steam to the top of a highly regarded and incredibly fruitful hedge fund in lower Manhattan. Nobody could blame him for this. His weaponized silence and slow decision-making process made him the last to begin to climb the ladder but also made his ascent the sturdiest, and ultimately, the longest. His peers revered him as a native negotiator, and he was applauded and awarded for his conscientious, unselfish business tactics. His career moved steadily upward like this for decades until Charles became the top, and there was nothing exciting left to do but look down. This meant that the business colleagues and loved ones he'd carried up with him had nowhere to look but to Charles, and like the face one sees after looking in a mirror too long, they began to see only the worst in him. All the things he fought for – enterprise, charity, collective well-being – began to antagonize the people in his life who saw it all as cannon fodder for the means that made the man. He became the root of so much projected disgust for his wives and his fellow businessmen that eventually they wanted nothing more than to see him perish. In all of Charles' unblemished morality, he had failed to see his deterioration in their eyes, failed to understand the motives of those around him, and didn't think to stop them before they could sink their teeth in.

The beginning of the end was a meeting six months earlier in the very same penthouse where Charles now grieves his mistakes. A long-time friend and business partner who Charles mistakenly trusted, who he affectionately referred to then as K.B., had been welcomed into Charles' home with a business proposition. K.B., associate manager of a less prominent but still somewhat fruitful hedge fund based in southern Rhode Island, came to Charles as a friend in need, as so many before him had, claiming that Charles was the only person who could help him. K.B.'s problem, as he enumerated to Charles from the very seat Alan now shuffles the deck of subpoenas, was that his fund's portfolio had become stretched extremely thin by a series of poor investment decisions – which he admitted were in large part his very own desperate mistakes. K.B. continued to claim that he was coming scarily close to being voted out of his position by the board as "negligent" and would need nothing short of an act of God to save him from the results of his own bad judgment. His god was now Charles, who held in his own personal portfolio a respectable share of Catharsis Insurance, a national brand name with an inescapable jingle that rang bells across America, and K.B. was enough of a long-time compatriot of Charles' to now comfortably beg that he lend those shares to K.B.'s hedge fund in exchange for K.B.'s most sincere appreciation (and a collateral letter of credit). K.B. relayed in quick succession that a) he would return the investment within three months because b) he would sell the shares at a lofty price and surely repurchase them soon after for pocket lint, which he claimed to know for a fact because he'd been c) "watching the stock for months, and could feel it was about to get caught in the inescapable suck of the trade floor toilet." To this, Charles assented. Not because he was getting older and was tired of foot-tapping in the open short position, not because he felt he was doing K.B. a favor for which he could be later rewarded, not because he thought K.B.'s argument was rock solid. Charles relented because he liked K.B. and thought he could help his friend.

After the short agreement was signed and the shares lent to K.B.'s hedge fund – not from Charles' fund but from his personal stock portfolio – it was only a matter of time before K.B.'s thickheaded plan blew up in both their faces. The fact was, K.B. hadn't been watching Catharsis' stock at all, but in fact was long-time croquet partners with Catharsis' CFO Farragut Chuck, who, in between strokes on the green, let out a burly, straight-from-the-colon type sigh before foolishly telling K.B., who he too considered his friend, that his company's days as the nation's catchiest insurance brand were numbered. Acting upon this kind of restricted information, K.B., who truly was under fire from his board of directors, was engaging in what the financial industry termed insider trading, and it served as the death-bringer of many a trader before him. So two months after that fateful meeting, when news broke that Catharsis Insurance had been forcing thousands of clients to pay for bogus coverage they could never hope to see the benefits of, and a fleet of lawsuits caused its stock price to plummet to a sixth of what it had been when K.B. sold the shares Charles had lent him, and K.B. had successfully shorted the stock and returned to his hedge fund's board with the ass-saving news, alarm bells rang across the table and the inevitable question was asked: "How Did You Know?" It took two months for the true details of K.B.'s short to completely unfold – in the form of investigative articles in *The Providence Journal* and then later on the web-edition of the genuine *Journal*, and Charles was named in both stories as a key party who had declined to comment. It goes without saying that K.B. was beelined for a white-collar prison stint and canonized across Facebook timelines as the new face of Wall Street getting what it deserved, as well as that the returns K.B. had received from selling Charles' shares were liquidated and sold back to Catharsis (who inevitably put them toward paying gigantic fines) and the collateral promise he made to Charles was never fulfilled.

Charles' carelessness, which led to innumerably lousy press for his hedge fund and the complete dissolution of K.B.'s was seen by many as a sign that his abilities were fading with age. On top of this, he was faced with a D.A. who knew that bringing down a big-name moneyman like Charles would paint him as the hero of the working class. Nonetheless, Charles couldn't be immediately criminally charged the way K.B. had, because in all his idiocy, K.B. was still kind to him in stating on police record that Charles had no idea about the information K.B. had, and was essentially a big fat dope that K.B. had swindled. In many ways, Charles *was* a big fat dope, in the way that overly generous people who blindly trust their friends inevitably turn out to be big fat dopes.

A triangulation of mutterings carves across the garbage fire like intersecting smores sticks.

"But so you tell me. What is it. Who's the whats."

"It's been told, Rico. Not gonna say it again."

"Yessir you gonna Tom cuz I asked. You wanna make me ask again?"

"You is askin' again righnow! It's like third time you ask me."

"There ain't gonna be a fourth 'fyou keep up."

"Lasko P.T.'s who's the deal with. He want the rock and tells me he pay a right price. He ain't gonna need it much longer so he say get right before Friday."

"When's that."

"Think'n two days."

"We gonna get it. We gonna get it."

"But what's it? What's the what?"

"E.Z. shut up. You think you don't know for a reason?'

"Couldn't see why. I ought to know."

"You deserve a pipe to the dome, E.Z. Keep shut."

'Tom. Tom. You keep shut. E.Z. is right. He ought to know."

"You tell him then."

"Please do, Rico. 'ppreciate chou."

"E.Z. You don't know cuz you be going out every day copping these 'zines, which you know we 'ppreciate, is why we where we is now and it's good. Tom and I been talkin' about doing something big. Making things right."

"Damn straight."

"You see that corner park with the big ugly mother fucker up tall?"

"I know it well. Adam Smith."

"That's right. So me and Tom thinkin' that corner park always empty. Nobody even go there on nice days. We bet nobody even notice that statue go missin'. Tom say that his boy Lasko P.T. cop that statue off us for Five together, Seven in pieces."

"He want the statue in pieces?"

"It ain't about the statue. It's 'bout the marble it's made of. 'pparently Tom's boy Lasko got a good gig dishing marble."

"Real good gig. Dishes to Eastern Euro builders who use it for rich family kitchen tops. Lasko says he get us Seven for the straight rock. Doesn't matter how it look."

"Seven's a lot of green. Do a lot in a lot like yours with Seven, Rico."

"Exacto E.Z. Exacto. That's why we need to bust that thing open and dish the parts to Lasko P.T. 'fore Friday. And you know what, I think you just the man to do it."

"You think I'm just the man for what."

"Bust that body wide open. I'll even front the cash to cop a sack of dirt bomb for you. I know a guy with connects by Holland Tunnel."

"Dirt bomb?"

"Shit bomb. Bomb o' dirt. It's this kind of fertilizational dirt. Light it up, and it blow fat. I say we stick a bag of that under Adam Smith's nut sack and collect what's left."

"When?"

"Tomorrow 'round sunset."

"Aight. I'll do it."

"Thattaboy, E.Z. This why you my boy. This why."

"Good shit E.Z., I'll tell Lasko tomorrow we getting right."

"And imma get you that shit bomb before you get back coppin' 'zines."

"Alright boys. Alright."

E.Z., which stands for Enzo, is not one to disappoint the friends who took him in, and has also developed his own reasons for wanting the statue destroyed. Following their agreement, Rico's lot turns noiseless but for the crackle of the flames, without even the fleeting sounds of rats scurrying in the shadows. The night sky is painfully clear.

The next day was slow and ruminative for E.Z., until it wasn't. Returning to Rico's lot with that day's magazine loot tucked between shoulder and side, he quickly saw that things were not the way they typically had been. Tom was aggressively performing what looked like half-understood yoga positions on a stack of material, and Rico was scribbling viciously on a piece of frayed cardboard.

"E.Z.! Com'ere righnow," Rico yelled as Tom restructured himself.

Rico displayed his scribbles for E.Z., which appeared to illustrate Rico's lot and the park, with a line drawn between both.

"This us. This where you gonna be when you drop the dirt bomb. This the way you should run after you light it. Keep runnin' 'til you can't hear no sirens. Don't come back here 'til night."

"Aight."

"Tom and me gonna be right behind you to collect the marble. We runnin' straight off the other way after that. All works out, we meet back here tonight with Seven."

"Aight."

Rico handed E.Z. a small plastic bag filled with what looked and smelled like dog shit. Inside were protruding pieces of paper meant to be lit as a makeshift fuse. He then handed E.Z. the lighter, which was white, with its designed wrapping peeled off.

"It's like sparkin' a doobie, except after you spark it, you run. Ain't no smoking this doobie."

"I ain't tryna smoke a doobie made of shit."

"That's right. You smart, E.Z.," Rico said.

"Good shit, E.Z," Tom agreed.

The sun mid-set overhead, Enzo moved briskly across the street and toward the park, his jeans sagging and wrapping around the soles of his shoes, ingraining the fibers of pant with who knows what under there, becoming a muggier and almost separate entity than the rest of his jeans. He floated between trees and cars like a cloud through a river valley, molding to the shape of the objects around him. Enzo was a stealth master, part of why he was so good at copping magazines. Gripping the bag loosely in a right hand covered by the end of his long sleeve, he looked right to left before approaching the statue and lighting the fuse. Rico and Tom crouched hidden behind an SUV at the corner, boxes and bags in hand.

It's impossible to know for sure if what happened next was simply a mirage, a case study of collective misremembering, or a genuine full-blown act of God. The empty street had meant there would be no direct witnesses besides Tom and Rico to agree that, in fact, the dirt bomb had blown, rather exceptionally at that, and been the cause of white marble flying every which way. There would be only parallel parkers who later found holes in their passenger side windows to confirm that, in fact, marble had been blown. There would be no definitive conclusion about how or why what happened happened, but it would be an element of folklore for many trash-fire discussions to come.

E.Z. didn't care to look back, but remembers hearing the sound as he ran randomly in the wrong direction away from a short fuse, and to his mind, that was enough. What he didn't see as he hopped a small fence and ran through a kimchee-infused alley behind Wae Woo's Korean and Noodle was perhaps the first and last genuine act of God. Because the dirt bomb had worked and had blown the white marble plinth to smithereens, but somehow, some way, the statue didn't blow. For some unidentifiable mystic reason, Adam Smith's black marble figure was completely intact from head to toe, and what's more, it didn't even fall. Adam Smith, the father of economics, just floated in mid-air without even the slightest rumble or shake, as if still rooted in the park. He was certainly floating, as Tom and Rico both later attested that the base he no longer stood on was crushed and sent flying in small bits throughout the park. But Adam, good old Mr. Smith, was secure, immovable. This is something E.Z. didn't see. What's worse was that the statue seemed to be rising, as if freed from its tie to the ground, slowly climbing higher into the air. This was a point heavily argued between Rico and Tom above later trash fires. The point that neither argued was that something happened there in that corner park that was worth immeasurably more than Seven. They knew something nobody else knew, and they believed it, bringing Rico and Tom closer than they ever could have thought.

What none of them knew was what was written on the backside of the marble base they destroyed, the side facing away from Rico's lot. On that side of the base, in small lettering, a quote from the father of economics was etched – before it was divided into chunks across the corner:

All money is a matter of belief.
–Adam Smith

Alan was a clinical worrier, but Charles' mind was made up. It seemed as though the limited decisions he had left to make about how he ended up had frozen him solid, and he stood staring out the window at the depths of New York, exactly as he had the day before. Alan, while no longer physically behind him, was worriedly ranting to Charles over speakerphone, his tone much different today than it had been.

"Those slimy, gutless bastards. They don't know what's coming to them, Charles. I'm going to fight this with everything I've got. These are inexcusable actions, totally blasphemous, and I'm going to make them choke on their words. Fire you? Fire *you*? What gives them the right? And of all things, for *negligence*? It's plainly unbelievable, and we're going to fight. Yes, we're going to fight, and we're going to win. You say the word, and I'll file the suit."

But Charles was getting older, and he knew in his heart that the time was right, whether it was his choice or theirs.

He knew he wasn't a negligent manager, but he had made his mistake and enabled the takers. He could no longer gather the power to even blame the vultures for picking at his bones, let alone fight, and was finally ready to let himself be killed.

"*Stare decisis*, Alan. *Stare decisis*."

Alan, an educated man, knew from television that when Latin was invoked, it meant the end was truly near.

"But the takers, we can't let the takers win. You said it yourself."

It's true. Charles didn't want to let the takers win. His sense of moral goodness had held firm, and he despised the notion that his role might be filled by a spineless money-grubbing monster – what he had seen so many of his colleagues become over the years. But powerlessness was powerlessness, and he knew he couldn't fight the board and win.

"*Stare decisis*," and he hung up on Alan for the very first time.

His "decision to step down," as the board had said he should term it, would create an opportunity for the advancement of hundreds of his former employees. So many hopeful newcomers fighting to climb their own ladders would now find themselves a rung higher, invigorating a new entrepreneurial spirit in the fund. The fund would most likely function better than it ever had under Charles, with a younger, more assertive and in-tune manager at the helm. The board would return to a state of passive comfort and assure the shareholders that their money would be safe.

Charles organized his own small stack of files and laid them on the great table, dwarfed by Alan's accumulation of worried notes. He laid down and penned his name to two documents, first the finalization of his divorce papers with the impenetrable C, divulging to her a great sum of his wealth, and then his will, which bequeathed his remaining fortune to his estranged son Enzo, who'd alienated himself from an upbringing of riches in search of a more fulfilling life.

Charles had always praised his son's moral sense, and prided himself on the thought that it was inherited. This illustrated to him a spirit that was worth the investment. His only concern was that his long-lost son, estranged for so long from a father who represented everything he despised, would find his sense of goodness corrupted by the sudden influx of wealth.

Charles kept this notion of corrupted morality in mind, but didn't think of it as he sent his head crashing through the window. No, as Charles began to descend the long way to the street below, he couldn't help but consider how all his actions, all the choices he had made to get where he was, were for the betterment of self. His self-interest was what ultimately guided him to the ground, and what inevitably left everyone around him far better off.

An invisible hand, orchestrating life after death.

11

Raisin Box

The way I see it is I just like things other people don't like. It's not their fault for not liking the same things I like, just like it's not mine I do. Everyone's got their own set of wishes and wants in the world, so that's not even an issue for me in the slightest. I guess the part of it that crunches my cylinders is how occasionally, not every time but some of the times, when you explain to them how you think about a certain thing or what your particular take on that specific area of life is, they think it's fair to pass a sideways look.

Let me say it again because it's got to be totally clear that I typically couldn't be bothered to even waste a breath on the thoughts or feelings of others. You know it just isn't my social style or how I present myself to the world. But with that being said, there are times when someone says or looks a certain way – maybe it's this upraised eyebrow some get or a kind of wince-like grin that puts me off into this otherworldly type of mood. That really takes me right out of my special social self and gives me this awfully coarse feeling inside, like I haven't got the space to be the way I'd like to. Because everyone knows the drill on how others feel about you. It's great to be open and willing to hear them out and listen to what they've got to say because we all know we're social animals. We're told that praise should be accepted and appreciated but not clung to, and criticism the same. But I guess I struggle with behaving the same way or responding the same way to two completely different emotional impulses.

For instance, and this is just an example, and by no means the reason why I'm off like this; it just came to mind. Horace Haversnacks, floor manager at work, who always wears the green suspenders and the clickety-clackety shoes that make you want to dance when you hear 'em. So Horace was clickety-clacking through the range at work and snuck up on my station out of the blue. And I'm all sweaty and bent up and hunched over the cradle working, not ever expecting Haversnacks to give me the light of day like he did, so you could say I was a little shocked when his green suspenders poked out over the cube-set. Well, first I saw the shoes, but then the suspenders. So well, at that point, I'm not looking or feeling my best, it's been a long day, and I hadn't gotten to lunch since Francis Yorkinsa caught bird flu and asked me to cover her at the desk. So when floor manager Haversnacks peered over my workstation and asked me how the weather was down there, I couldn't really feel my throat or face. So this isn't a typical feeling I get, but you know, once in a while, when the workload is really heavy and everything sort of gets warm throughout my insides. I had to spit, essentially. But Horace wanted to know the weather. I said it was alright and I could use a break, so he said sure. Don't ask me what happened in the bathroom. It became awfully clear I wasn't going back to work for a little while after that one.

GINSBERG

Well I guess I forgot where I was in my story because what I was trying to tell you was how different my interests are from those of other people, and that's really the point I'm going to get to. The dust-up with Haversnacks and the desecration of the lavatory floor was almost a fluke, but it had to be mentioned for reasons you'll soon know. So where was I? Oh, right, off about the idea of having different sorts of likes and dislikes than any other body, and how it couldn't matter less what they say or think or feel about it until it does.

Because whether you like it or not, the mailman eventually starts knocking on your door. After a while, once the mailbox is overflowed and they haven't got a safe place to stick the letters, they knock and holler and try to get you to open and take the stuff. I guess it's in their job description to be sure that you'll get the stuff when it's meant to get delivered. But how's a mailman supposed to know it's not right to knock and holler when it's in their job description? That's why I really can't blame them, even though I'd love to be able to. There's another cerebral doozy I find myself consistently troubled by.

So about a week after they first knock and holler, you might feel like you should poke a head out and just mention that the doorstep's fine and you'll get to it in a bit, but that means brushing your hair down and wiping your eyes and clearing the snot from your jacket and such. Which is just such a hassle considering the difficulty of even getting up off the rocking chair. So I split the difference, put together a little note, and tacked it onto the front door. If I remember right the note said something like the doorstep's fine. So lucky me the mailman didn't holler back again, and I'm glad for that.

Well about a month passed before I could go back to work at the cradle bunker. That's what we called it because you couldn't get in or out of that place without a damn good reason to be there. That's just the way Haversnacks liked it, and I damn well respected Haversnacks for that position. So I was at home for a month or a month plus some just wasting away, snotting all over my jacket and spitting in cups for no reason other than they were close by. I hadn't even the time or energy to make it to the grocer, so I had to pull all the fruit and eggs and bread and milk and cheese from the fridge in the kitchen and bring them back over by the rocking chair so that a week or two weeks later when I knew I wasn't going to have the energy to get to the kitchen I could just pick myself up a bread and cheese sandwich from the chairside table. Which was a great idea but until obviously once the food starts to get rotten and the figs start smelling like sour onion and everything just gets really nasty, and it stops being cozy at all in the room. And then the rats come in and start mowing away at your rotten lunch, and Haversnacks hasn't had the chance to check up on your desk in a little while, and you miss the sound of those clickety-clacking shoes of his and the smell of the fresh tweed cradle when it's new off the vine, and you start to think your mailman is suspicious you're dead and it's all for damn Francis Yorkinsa and that damn bird flu she left over at the desk.

So I still don't really agree with the likes and dislikes of other people, and now I'll start to tell you why. Because after a while you start to get really comfortable with the rats and the mow and the smell of rotten onion, and why? Because it starts to feel like home. Because you start to feel like damn, if I'm going to smell like rotten onion and be too far away from the floor for so long that Haversnacks probably forgets I even exist and starts hovering over someone else's desk asking about the weather than maybe I deserve to be here. Maybe it's right that I got Yorkinsa's leftover bird flu and can't get up off my rocking chair. But that's a toxic way to feel after just three and a half weeks of not leaving the room and pissing all over yourself. And I don't think it's toxic because someone else told me it was or because you think it is, but because I made the personal decision to believe it's that way. That's part of my point.

But the rest of my point is that once you start to feel down in the dumps and sick and filthy like that and before you get the chance to pick yourself up by your skirt straps you got to hit rock bottom. I mean always. That's just the way I see it. So rock bottom for me was the raisin trap. Because after everything in the fridge has been taken out, and everything that's been taken out has gone bad, there are very few things a sick and filthy young girl can eat from her chair but raisins. And I'm not necessarily proud of how this shook out exactly, but I'd like to make it totally clear that the idea was based on good faith and the execution was almost exact.

So at this point, you're obviously wondering what on earth I am talking about when I say raisin trap. Well, the idea was simple and caused by the fact that rats don't sleep quiet. If you've ever heard or seen a rat sleep, you'll know that they wince and whimper like little chew toys when they snooze. I couldn't say why. I'm no rat expert. What I am is a woman who loves to get a little bit of rest in and who simply can't do so with a gaggle of huddling vermin squeezing and squishing around like rubber duckies just beside her. So the raisin trap was a sort of simple idea, and it was a good way to get me up and off my rocking chair. Basically what happened was I set up a sort of pulley system, which after getting yanked would trigger a snatch harness, which would rope around this box of raisins I had placed precariously on the table ledge, and that raisin box would hit the floor hard by where the rats slept. But the first pulley wasn't set up to get yanked by me, I had it placed so that the rats would do it by accident if they tried to get back up to the fruit and cheese and bread I had on the table. So basically, if one of those squimpering rodents wanted to get greedy and filthy on my pile of goods, they were putting the lives of their fellow vermin at risk. And that was a great way to get me up off my chair and feeling better.

But I got into a real rock-hard place type deal when only one rat was left because all his buddies got squashed by the raisin trap. What am I going to do about one rat left if there's no way to get him sleeping and eating at the same time? So I just yanked the damn thing myself while he was squimpering and that was that.

Which reveals to you the ultimate point of why I started off on this bit in the first place, which I really didn't want to do but felt like I had to since you seemed so destitute and clueless and out of touch with what was really important. What you need to know and what I had to learn the really really hard way after about a month of filthy sitting pissing and rat handling is that whatever you do and however you choose to do it, ultimately, is your choice. Other people will look at you, sniff at you, and maybe even raise an eyebrow, but have they walked in your shoes? What can they say about you that you haven't already thought and discounted in your own head? Nothing, that's the point. You can have your own interests and likes and dislikes, and other people can have theirs. So if they ever snicker or gossip or give you bird flu or stop coming by your desk to ask about the weather or eventually fire you and call you a smelly rat-lady, you should remember that.

12

Excerpts from "I Come To Heal"

a story I may never be done with

Mona Lisa

An unhappy person is a beautiful thing, if made right. Cynicism can be beauty. Pessimism can be beauty. Dissatisfaction can be beauty. The same way that thunderclaps and lightning storms make for marvelous paintings. Think Mona Lisa. Think Shakespeare. Think Sophocles. In the western world, tragedies make up 75 percent of a child's required reading. The West is addicted to tragedies in its books, shows, films, myths, newspapers, and religions. It loves tragedy when it strikes at a grand scale – the killed politician, the disgraced A-lister. The Westerner wants to be affected. She wants to be stricken. She wants to be shocked, mesmerized and entertained. She wants to gossip. She wants to feel scarred, wounded, and burnt. She wants to feel like she feels it more deeply and more truly than anyone else. She wants to use tragedy as a reminder to love authentically and love always. To grow closer than ever to the people she loves. She wants to mourn, but she also wants to recover, and to be the last of her circle to do so. She wants to forget, to move on, to have grown in some meaningful way. She wants this cycle to repeat itself over and over and over again, but she doesn't want to admit that. She wants tragedy to strike constantly, so much so that she can pick and choose which tragedies to focus her attention on. And when there's no tragedy in the news, she wants it in her TV shows and music. She wants to feel. She wants to be close to something. She wants everyone she knows to also know what tragedy feels like, and for it to represent something powerful and mature and unique about them. Part of her wants the power of tragedy to reach everyone everywhere, so they too can grow in this way. She wants tragedy to touch all the way it has touched her. She wants tragedy at a distance, somewhere she can see and pull close. She doesn't want it at her front door.

Rarely, she might let herself fantasize about what her friends might think if tragedy ever struck her directly. She might wonder if they would mourn her or pray for her. She might contemplate what specific brand of tragedy she'd prefer if she were destined to suffer one. She might prefer something medical, something serious and life-threatening. Big enough to make people she only tangentially knows really *feel*. But something with a cure. Something hopeful – because she'd want to survive. She'd want to have the types of conversations that people who survive big medical emergencies get to have. At least the types they have on TV. She'd want the person she'd always secretly admired to show up after the tragedy is over and tell her he'd been praying for her the whole way through. She'd want to brush her tragedy off over time, not draw the thing out too much after the fact. Let other people bring it up. What wouldn't kill her would make her stronger. She'd mature. Become harder but not hard. She'd be able to give advice to people and feel justified in doing so. She'd have the satisfaction of having faced something, of having overcome it, and having become better for it. She'd be storied. She'd be recognized. She'd be the person she knows she could be. She hopes to become that person anyway, even if tragedy never strikes her. But maybe that's what tragedy is for. Maybe that's why she's so drawn to it.

Unhappy people don't become unhappy overnight. They're worked, pressured, pressed like glass at the furnace. The truth about tragedy is that it's almost never sexy and almost never makes the news. It's routine, rote. It's an unsatisfying marriage. A car crash on the interstate. A teen pregnancy. Most tragedies don't come with a complicated backstory that's fleshed out delicately through rising action. They don't come with an omniscient narrator. They don't come with comedic relief. They come quietly. And more often than not, they go that way too. It's worst when a child is born out of tragedy and predestined for more. Worse still if they don't even know it.

Pain

Pock.

Be careful when smothering your pain with violence. Unlike hiding it under calm or disregarding it through fake-smile extroversion, violence has the unforgiving ability to broadcast your pain to the outside world. Common examples include: revenge, religious acts of terror (particularly when directed against the sexually free), most forms of civil war, just about every case of domestic violence, and bar fights started over women who thought their man knew he was loved. It should be noted that not *all* violence is a direct manifestation of smothered pain. Sometimes violence is purely retaliatory. Sometimes it's enacted for the greater good. Though these are rare cases, and often simply justifications or excuses.

Tip-Tap-Tip. Pock. Tap-Tip. Poom-Pock.

The external suffering caused by violence set aside, there are other reasons to avoid broadcasting your pain to the outside world. Namely, that pain is infectious, and letting it bleed out of the crevices of your own mind can often lead to the slow and painful degradation of otherwise untouched aspects of your world. Let one thing be clear – this is not an invitation to bottle your pain. Try that and watch as your insides rot like a berry in the sun. No. Better to let your pain live and breathe in controlled environments – where it can bounce from wall to wall and linger in the air. Introduce it to every corner of your little room. Let it hang like mist and stink up the place. Growth is what it feels like to sit there, breathing all that in, day after day. It's resisting the urge to crack a window.

Slip-Whoosh-Poom. Tap-Tap-Tap-Tip. Pock-Whoosh-Poom.

Avoid paying for therapy in almost all cases. Every therapist will tell you that their job isn't to solve your problems for you but to guide you along the way toward solving them yourself. Resist guidance as a disguise for control. By all means, if you've found yourself in such a deep and dark hole that the only way out of it, save death, is to grab an outstretched hand – grab it. But do everything you can, when you can, to let it go. Not because your therapist can't help you. Not because therapy isn't good, useful, or worthwhile. But because the resonant awareness of that always-available hand will never leave you – and will wedge itself right between you and recovery *for all time.* The caterpillar becomes a butterfly on its own accord, entirely within a darkened, isolated pupa. This can take weeks, months, years. Never is too long.

Have deep and difficult conversations with yourself. Stop thinking it's too hard, or unfair, or that you can't be objective when analyzing your pain and how it manifests. The first rule of objectivity is, disappointingly, that you alone are the arbiter of what is and isn't objective for you. You might call that subjectivity – but at the end of the day, you can be just as objective about your own suffering as someone else. Probably more. But don't get distracted by the terms and conditions of it all. This isn't objectivity in the grand scheme. This has nothing to do with universal equations or the fabric of consensus reality. This is just you, alone in your own dark head, answering real, hard problems – not to free yourself from the questions themselves, but to one day convince those questions to drop their weapons.

Tap. Poom.

It's easy to dismiss this initial idea as unforgivingly stoic, macho, and unsympathetic. This urge arises from our deep, maternalistic yearning to ease the pain of others and ourselves. To lighten it, loosen its grip. This is not a bad thing. In cases where one's energy is spread too thin across the multitude of stresses, worries, and annoyances of daily life, it can even be the right thing. Though these dismissals will always catch up with you over a long enough time frame. In the end, dismissal of one's own responsibility for healing is just another form of pain.

Pock.

Tap.

Poom.

13

Decided To Live Today

In the building that faces my bedroom window work roughly four hundred people. Office types with smirks and quivers, built into squares, their shadows descending long from their black and normal swivel chairs. It rises high, the building does, carving cracks in clouds of metallic blue, reflecting heat and steam as they rise, searching slowly for sweet release. The windows are all the same size and very big, much larger than need be for the office types to smirk and look down at the DieCast Playset traffic clotting far below. There's a room in the corner that must be reserved because it's never filled, likely saving air for a very rich and thoroughly regular man when he finds time to respirate there. When it rains, the drops coagulate into a million scattered thought bubbles on the long matted windows, dripping and sliding and swishing around until there's not much left inside to see. Once, a raincloud hung so low above the roof that the building looked comically troubled indeed.

I can see this all from my bedroom window, and it never changes – just a constant shuffling from left to right, like an airport's moving-sidewalk stuffed with business-casual chickens coasting headless through their maze of sad (which they navigate by muscle memory), and I can see this all from my bedroom window just across the street, knowing they could see me too if they ever ripped their eyes away from their memos or fax machine spew and looked up over and across the way, which they rarely, if ever, do.

I'm standing straight up naked with my nuts out facing my wall-sized bedroom window, wearing a watch. Conducting a social experiment, a little test I've had on my mind for far too long now. There's a tall glass of water on the desk beside the window for if I get thirsty, and I made sure to eat well before I got going. I ate eggs with ketchup and challah bread to soak the juice, because no bread soaks the juice the way that challah bread does. So with my tummy feeling swell and my nuts hangin' low, I stand, for the last 42 minutes 11 seconds, waiting for something to happen. I figure that once it's been an hour I'll take a quick bathroom break, but then it's back to nut hanging water sipping time recording. I'm chewing mint gum, for the freshness.

At 24 minutes, I began to feel a slight twinge in my back, which I resolved over the course of two and a half minutes of side-to-side twisting and bending, because there's nothing more resolute than the snap and release of a well-executed back crack. This is a social experiment. What I really want to know is how long before an over-qualified, under-utilized intern gazes hopefully out the window, and their line of sight catches no less than, yes, my nuts, hanging low. How long before their jaw drops and their muscle memory fades, and they yell something like:

"*Ah!*"

Or you know like even a gasp maybe:

"*Ooh!*"

How long before said intern reveals their view to the other regulation chicken office headless types with their smirks and quivers, and they all creep slowly toward the big window like it's roadkill, cup their hands around their eyes and find they too have none other than a clear image of guess what? My nuts, hanging low. How long before one of them decides to do something about it? What exactly does one do in a situation like that? This is a social experiment.

14

Brought To You By Big Dairy

I

And having got himself on death row, as one does, was a difficult task all its own. This one, Jamie Diamond, the rowed one, the one with no more than six minutes of life still to live, depending, sits shackled and braced for the wickedest of wicked, thinks of a day not more than four months prior. A passable-for-good weather day in July on the beach in Isla Coco, pre-noon, palm trees above head still dripping with the patient dew of the summer's fogged and winded night gone by. There on the beach – before the girl came back from the pasture and he hadn't yet heard the news, he sat similarly shackled, splayed between two palms like a loose hammock, wrists tied by a dry, splintering rope to an empty life-guard chair – his bare ass sanded like schnitzel and starting to itch. On this day, the visibility just par, he can see no further than the Gulf's nearest island, 450 meters due east, its patchy mangrove trees jutting like pimples above the shoreline. He watches an eagle cross over the grove, perch high, and call, which can't be true. By the time the girl returns from the pasture, he's already lost sensibility, plus there's sand in his ears.

"Chiquitito. No tenemos espacio para usted. Vete," the girl says, untying her naked visitor, leaving for the second time. Jamie flips cock-side and watches her gain distance, unsure what it is he has to say.

"Disculpe," he clamors before she's too far. "¿Cuál es el tiempo?"

"Qué hora es, gringuito. Qué hora es."

"¿Qué hora es?"

"Once. Once y media."

"Gracias."

"Con gusto, chiquitito." And she turns again, back to the pasture where her roots have been sown, where her people had buried her mother, where they would eventually bury her.

The sun rises higher in the sky, and will soon hit its midday peak, ready as a gavel to beat on Diamond's head. As he rises off his rump and hops with burnt feet to the now deflated raft he drifted in on, he wonders, feeling paranoid and cursed, if there are sprinkles in his future.

II

Diamond covers himself in a fallen palm leaf to guard against the sun, and looking like an ear of corn left unshucked, blows slow and deep to fill the raft. Once ready, he sets off from Isla Coco without looking back, into the Gulf where there is to be very little for him.

Above his head, the eagles couple and bunch, arranging themselves like chocolate sprinkles against the backdrop of the sun. With just his person and the three coconuts he had found littered on the beach, the raft is light on entertainment, so after cracking open the thickest one with a rock and guzzling it down, he dozes off. Occasionally he is woken at the call of a faraway bird, only to return again to sleep. There truly was very little for him out there that day in the Gulf, but for the knowledge that his days would get much worse before they got better, and too, the pinging, nagging possibility of sprinkles in his future.

Two decades before that day, Diamond's birthday in Kansas City, Missouri. He, his sister, and his mother walk two miles to get little Jamie a cone of vanilla from Baskin Robbins, then home to no more than 18 or so flavors. Had they not taken him to BR for celebration on b-day number 9, Jamie would have whelped and swung and broken things until something changed. Call that the first time someone should have glimpsed violence in his future, but of course no one did, which brings us back to where we are now.

Four months after that hot day in the Gulf off Isla Coco, in the holding cell where he will later be electrified into a state of death, Jamie Diamond hopes and prays to his sweet and merciful lord and savior Jesus Almighty Christ that there won't be sprinkles. Just a level below, one Truman Pooce, night guard at Crickman Holding and Detention Facility in Corpus Christie, Texas, where the residential obese population rarely dips below cone-dropping levels, Pooce, who's just around bigfoot-type size, walks down the underground hallway of Crickman H&D toward an elevator.

In his left hand, Pooce delicately grasps a vanilla ice cream cone, intent not to crush the nimble, flaky crust with the overstuffed chorizos he calls fingers, walking with locked knees and big eyes focused dearly on the petite cone. He notices a little bit of vanilla drip over the side, and it's getting on his pointer finger, and some irrational panic pings him in the side of the head. This throws him off as he reaches the elevator, as his distracted mind leads him to attempt to push the UP button with his cone-wielding hand, throwing the top orb of the double-scoop cone into motion, a motion he fights by quickly flicking his wrist down and out, a momentous maneuver that sends his whole Big & Tall person into whiplash, cracking him at the hips and landing him kneeling on the floor.

Luckily, the cone is saved. From his holy Islamic position, he presses UP with the crown of his nose. He plans to wait until the elevator arrives, when he will make use of the space between the elevator car and the elevator shaft to get a grip with his right hand and pull-assist his way back onto his feet. All this while keeping Pro Bowler-like focus on the traumatized cone in his left. By now, his paranoia is replaced with submissiveness, as he is cornered by the will of a slowly melting vanilla cone, something this behemoth of a man has grown to understand quite well over the years. A cone-fearing man whose life now rests wholly in the hands of his sugary temptation, "hands" also literal, as the sticky iced cream continues to drip down the side of his outer left hand's grip, soon to make a landing on his wedding ring.

As the elevator dings and its door opens and Pooce is meant to get in that car and end the drama, the climax extends as his dilemma grows from what now seems so trivial – getting on his feet while maintaining balance of cone – to now all of that, plus keeping the drip of the cream from damaging his most valuable token of love from his dear wife Darlene, his platinum wedding ring – now just seconds away from being coated white with vanilla destruction. He motions to move the cone to his right hand but freezes once he realizes that immobilizing that hand would leave him without the means to pull-assist himself to his feet.

Defeated, totally without option, Pooce makes the hasty and ill-advised move to sacrifice his ring, clasp onto the elevator, rise to his feet, get in the car, transition the cone from left hand to right, and examine the damage. His fear is realized, and boy won't Darlene get done up about this.

III

As the elevator struggles against the weight of our man Truman Pooce, he is recovering from yet another ping to his temple.

See, as he'd been kneeling, the circulation cut off from his lower legs, so when he stood, blood rushed down to fill his trousers, so much and so quickly that his brain temporarily lost its fill, and he got hit with a rush of light and dizziness that left him unable to see or coordinate. Unfortunately for Pooce, he'd already been on the way to pushing the L1 button when this all hit him, so his weariness guided him in as he finished the forward motion, accidentally pushing the ALARM WILL SOUND button and getting up-ended by a striking, painfully loud "WEAWEAWEAWEAWEAWEA," followed by a jolt as the car stopped midway between B and L1. So now, as the disorientation eases away from the center of his vision, Pooce fully realizes what's just happened. He presses for HELP and, being hit repeatedly by the biting ping of the ringing alarm, while still recovering from cardio-circular distress, begins to feel sorry for himself. Sorrow for oneself is a curse for a man of his size, and, predictably, for his troubles, Pooce has a lick of a vanilla ice cream cone that was never meant for him.

In another world, four months prior, this: lyrically speaking, it's hard to pin down why Diamond sings this particular song to the pirates who find him slowly sinking in the Gulf of Mexico, but the facts don't lie:

O Dios Mío, make me your meat man,
Leave me corroding, funky, and fed up
Uncle, oh uncle, call me the Graced one.
Terms and conditions, despite that I've been found
Drip me in orange, peach me a mango
Audible, obvious, you've made me mistaken.

Of course, the pirates speak about enough English to catch no percent of that, but it doesn't matter; Diamond speaks to himself. They'd saved him, searched him, found nothing of worth, and shackled him by the neck to a flag post. The ship's captain had cut into one of the coconuts they'd taken from the raft, drank half and threw the empty shell overboard. (That coconut would later float to the Arctic, stupefying a gaggle of penguins (as coconuts sometimes do)). The captain says nothing to Diamond as he squats down and looks him in the eye, then down at his chest. He takes off his hat, tosses it over Diamond's cock, turns around, and shouts something incomprehensible to his crew.

Diamond can't stop repeating the song's second verse, amusing himself for no reason other than that his brain is slowly bubbling to a hot soup. Could he find a way off the ship? The knot around his wrists is corrosively tight, but the hat on his cock gives him some hope. He thinks about the possibility of having a drink, and carries a soft call to the nearest seaman.

"Padre."

A thumb-sized individual in button shorts and a loose-necked rag turns and points a cutting stare at Diamond. He takes three steps forward and squats.

"Qué?"

"Usted, y yo."

"Y yo?"

"Si. Usted. Y yo."

Diamond widens his leg toward the seaman, letting the hat fall a touch inward. The seaman spins his head around, thinks twice, and replies swift and firm.

"Después."

"Ahora."

It's tough to say exactly why the seaman thought this could work, but again, the facts don't lie. The seaman returns to his post with a wink and waits until the captain and crew go down for a midday meal, then unclasps Diamond's shackle. Pulling down his trousers and grabbing Diamond by the ears, he makes the obvious, anticlimactic mistake of closing his eyes in an ill-conceived attempt to focus more on the feeling, which is, of course, when Diamond grabs the dagger from the seaman's hip and thrusts it into his abdomen, twisting the blade as he rises to his feet. Diamond eases him to the deck. Then, while the boy lies there slowly transmitting to invisibility, Diamond cuts the top off a coconut, drinks half, pours the other half into the faded seaman's mouth, and sets the shell down over his brazen cock, so, as Diamond later swore, on the off chance the seaman were to meet his Madre en Cielo, he could look her in the eye.

Meanwhile, well not really meanwhile, but four months in the future, Truman Pooce sits wide-kneed, waiting for help to arrive. His lips are sticky white with leftover cream and crumbs of cone, damage he inflicted on himself in a hasty attempt to quell nerves. Ill-advised, too, because soon, when he is inevitably saved, he'll have to look Chief Correctional Officer Quincy Duck in his face and explain why the ice cream is gone, cone and all, say "poof," where it went, why. He'll have to say something to account for the fact that another cone will need to be retrieved, possibly taking another 15 minutes to half an hour, depending on traffic, effectively pushing back the death-by-electrification to later that day. Pooce can picture the look on Duck's face when he tells him how it all went down, the ice cream elevator marital woe drama. It's a bad face.

So as Pooce waits for the electrician to come get his ass out the shaft, he runs the story over in his head systematically, painstakingly, thinking of how to frame it in as honest and sincere a form he can, all while his thoughts are interrupted by pings to his temple, resulting from of course the alarm & the future pain he'll be forced to lay out on Darlene, but also by the basically 100% chance that Duck, for one reason or another, will choose not to take Pooce's word for it and will check the B-level security cameras to confirm. That's Pooce's main fear, there on the car floor, which is why, holding a wide-kneed seated position for four minutes plus, the alarm ringing WEAWEAWEA directly over his head, he thinks hard and harder about whether to start his explanation with this:

"Duck, have some grace."

IV

Diamond is impatient as ever for the great sprinkle reveal. If he could, that is, if the straps were less tight and he had an inch to spare, he would literally be at the edge of his seat. He salivates. He measures minutes as they pass by the forward-backward pace of the man in front of him, a man who looks like a cliff – someone to be jumped off of. This person is by no mistake CCO Quincy Duck, who's pacing up and down the meat locker-sized, electromagnetically in-sealed room at roughly five second intervals there-and-back, so every twelfth time Duck hits the right wall, Diamond knows a minute's gone. Duck's hit the right wall about 168 times, so figure that one out if you care. If you don't, just know that it's been a little while here waiting, which is bad for the tempers in the room, particularly Duck's, who, for reasons unknown to him, always feels like he's got somewhere to be that's more narratively relevant than where he is now. The life of a risen and rising jailor in Texas, one presumes.

Meanwhile, four months prior and a few points down south, Diamond has just completed the cock-tease kill of this darling little Mexican. Trouble is, there's a gaggle of sword-wielding pirates on the deck below, and he's got to make off with the booty before they finish tea-time, except, where's the booty? The booty he came here with. The reason he's out in this body of water to start. The booty found not three days prior, 45 feet due East of the Southern reef of Isla Coco, fought for with a team of tiger sharks: earned booty. Booty with some legitimate historical value in the high-art circles of Chelsea, NYC. Diamond had had the booty, which made it legally his when he had it because of international waters, but where was it? Not here? Don't swivel your head and check the floor around your feet, idiot. Was it international waters? No. He stole it. He stole it, then shored up at Isla Coco having drowned. Must have been saved by the girl. He had the booty tied around his waist with some sea straw. Then there was the girl, but she didn't take it. Maybe, when she left the first time?

Somewhere in hyperspace, where time doesn't manufacture linguistic boundaries, and there's no need to use words like "two decades before" or "meanwhile" or "here and now," and where it's actually laughable to say a thing like "in another world," a fat slob with a shit marriage is helped out of an elevator. He hates himself and commits to telling Duck the entire, flimsy, almost forgotten story. He plans to *ask* for the security cam footage to be viewed, to accept its inevitable sharing between co-workers and subsequent

YouTube virality. He prays only that the commenters lend some credit to his having saved the ice cream, which may or may not cancel out the unavoidable replies to any such comment regarding how, to a man of Pooce's build, the cream was the only thing in life worth saving.

No commenter's mind will be paid to the fact that the ice cream was never event meant for Pooce, that it was really meant to end up in the hands of Jamie Diamond, internationally recognized treasure hunter, vigilante, trickster, cold killer, all of the above while also maximally handsome, sexy, appealing to mammals of all kinds and for all reasons, who's currently waiting in a meat-locker-sized room on the 1 Level of Crickman Holding & Detention Center in Corpus Christie, TX, not twenty yards from the elevator Pooce just broke, waiting for the thing he's been after since the very start, the booty above and away from all other booty, a vanilla ice cream cone, regular, hold the sprinkles.

V

On the ship, dead Mexican forgotten, Diamond, like a chess novice, plays the move that had his eye from the start. He pushes for the wheel to steer the ship off course.

Down below, the crew finishes up their tortas as they feel the boat begin to stir, and being Mexican Border Patrol officials, swiftly pursue and capture the young Jamie Diamond, the reality being that this is no pirate ship, they no pirates. Jamie had been so diluted and disheveled at the hand of the merciless post-noon sun that he'd conjured the whole thing up for good fun. En-ter-tain-ment. Ever heard of it? It used to exist once.

The crew gets him back in cuffs, all the tighter now that he's the murderer of future American sailor Brooklyn Quest, the murder which really did happen, not at all a part of Diamond's great imaginary narrative, because why would it be? Much too dark for a fantasy story.

So Quest, a once 19-year old pimple-ridden ROTC exchange kid from Fort Worth now had to be explained for, a total fucking major dolor de cabeza for Rigaldo Martinéz, Jefe del Programa de Cambio de Servicio Extranjero Mexicano, aka supervisor of god-damn mother-fucking Brooklyn Quest, the dead kid who a castaway tricked into murder by fellatio.

So long story short, Brooklyn Quest is, fortunately for Diamond, the only American citizen on the boat, which means his immediate extradition to Estados Unidos, an expedited trial and, for offing a troop-to-be in the surrounding area of the great American stronghold of Tejas, where the one thing you don't do is disrespect the armed forces, is sentenced to electrification until death by a jury of his peers. Which brings us right where we are.

Crickman H&D: Pooce Big & Tall gets an earful of fire from his personal Jefe Quincy Duck. Duck slips a disk from laughing so hard at Pooce's story. Pooce drinks the cocktail of embarrassment & humiliation, holds on to the lingering thought of his wife's face when she sees what he's done to her ring, seizes. Like, *has a seizure,* a consequence of which is that he throws up all over the electrification room floor; spills his guts like a firehose.

Meanwhile, here and now, in the very same room where this all occurs, where guts have just seconds ago been spilt, Jamie Diamond bursts into hysterical laughter. He shakes in his straps, veins popping from his neck, tongue taking on a life of its own in the world. He can't stop. He's in a different dimension of hysteria. His eyes water. He cries.

Because of course he knew he was on a Border Patrol boat, and that kid was an ROTC exchangee, and there was never any booty to start with. Diamond had always been a castaway, had always conjured stories to share with himself in the dark and damp annals of his mind. There was only that, his world, separate from all that was terrestrial, shared. In isolation, he'd manufactured and perfected a world of imaginary fantasy, where booty lay hidden around him all the time, ticking along its own mystic clock, aching to be searched for. It was a longing he harbored deep, the searching for – and the knowing that, along the way, coursing downstream on a river he'd carved for himself, he might find something known.

It just so happened that that thing was a vanilla ice cream cone, regular, hold the sprinkles, a memory within a memory. He'd found that comfort then, as a nine-year old, when all that mattered was the having. But now, looking down at a milky white floor, dotted with red, orange, green, purple and blue spots, he finds that all he ever cared for was the searching.

About the Author

Guy Ginsberg was born in Lod, Israel, in 1998 and raised in Beverly Hills, California. He received a bachelor of the arts degree in journalism from The George Washington University, where he began writing the stories that would make up this collection. Ginsberg is a musician (under the name *guydxnce*) and video producer as well as a writer, and is currently working on his first album and feature film. Decided to Live Today is his first collection of short fiction to be published. He lives in West Hollywood, California.